CHRISTOPHER BUSH
THE CASE OF THE HANGING ROPE

CHRISTOPHER BUSH was born Charlie Christmas Bush in Norfolk in 1885. His father was a farm labourer and his mother a milliner. In the early years of his childhood he lived with his aunt and uncle in London before returning to Norfolk aged seven, later winning a scholarship to Thetford Grammar School.

As an adult, Bush worked as a schoolmaster for 27 years, pausing only to fight in World War One, until retiring aged 46 in 1931 to be a full-time novelist. His first novel featuring the eccentric Ludovic Travers was published in 1926, and was followed by 62 additional Travers mysteries. These are all to be republished by Dean Street Press.

Christopher Bush fought again in World War Two, and was elected a member of the prestigious Detection Club. He died in 1973.

By Christopher Bush

The Plumley Inheritance
The Perfect Murder Case
Dead Man Twice
Murder at Fenwold
Dancing Death
Dead Man's Music
Cut Throat
The Case of the Unfortunate Village
The Case of the April Fools
The Case of the Three Strange Faces
The Case of the 100% Alibis
The Case of the Dead Shepherd
The Case of the Chinese Gong
The Case of the Monday Murders
The Case of the Bonfire Body
The Case of the Missing Minutes
The Case of the Hanging Rope
The Case of the Tudor Queen
The Case of the Leaning Man
The Case of the Green Felt Hat

CHRISTOPHER BUSH

THE CASE OF THE HANGING ROPE

With an introduction
by Curtis Evans

DEAN STREET PRESS

Published by Dean Street Press 2018

Copyright © 1937 Christopher Bush

Introduction copyright © 2018 Curtis Evans

First published in 1937 by Cassell & Co.

Cover by DSP

ISBN 978 1 911579 99 1

www.deanstreetpress.co.uk

DEDICATED

with sincere gratitude to

THE CRITICS

by a professional who in these days of amateur
competition is only too aware that it is better to be
cussed than ignored.

Every character, situation, place and incident
in this story is wholly imaginary.
The reader will even recognize that it is a
wholly imaginary B.B.C.

INTRODUCTION

THAT ONCE vast and mighty legion of bright young (and youngish) British crime writers who began publishing their ingenious tales of mystery and imagination during what is known as the Golden Age of detective fiction (traditionally dated from 1920 to 1939) had greatly diminished by the iconoclastic decade of the Sixties, many of these writers having become casualties of time. Of the 38 authors who during the Golden Age had belonged to the Detection Club, a London-based group which included within its ranks many of the finest writers of detective fiction then plying the craft in the United Kingdom, just over a third remained among the living by the second half of the 1960s, while merely seven—Agatha Christie, Anthony Gilbert, Gladys Mitchell, Margery Allingham, John Dickson Carr, Nicholas Blake and Christopher Bush—were still penning crime fiction.

In 1966--a year that saw the sad demise, at the too young age of 62, of Margery Allingham--an executive with the English book publishing firm Macdonald reflected on the continued popularity of the author who today is the least well known among this tiny but accomplished crime writing cohort: Christopher Bush (1885-1973), whose first of his three score and three series detective novels, *The Plumley Inheritance*, had appeared fully four decades earlier, in 1926. "He has a considerable public, a 'steady Bush public,' a public that has endured through many years," the executive boasted of Bush. "He never presents any problem to his publisher, who knows exactly how many copies of a title may be safely printed for the loyal Bush fans; the number is a healthy one too." Yet in 1968, just a couple of years after the Macdonald editor's affirmation of Bush's notable popular duration as a crime writer, the author, now in his 83rd year, bade farewell to mystery fiction with a final detective novel, *The Case of the Prodigal Daughter*, in which, like in Agatha Christie's *Third Girl* (1966), copious references are made, none too favorably, to youthful sex, drugs and rock and roll. Afterwards, outside of the reprinting in the UK in the early 1970s of a scattering of classic Bush titles from the Golden Age, Bush's books, in contrast with those of Christie, Carr, Allingham and Blake, disappeared from mass circulation in both the UK and the US, becoming fervently sought (and ever more unobtainable) treasures by collectors and connoisseurs of classic crime fiction. Now, in one of the signal developments in vintage mystery publishing, Dean Street Press is reprinting all 63 of the Christopher Bush detective novels. These will be published over a period of months, beginning with the release of books 1 to 10 in the series.

Few Golden Age British mystery writers had backgrounds as humble yet simultaneously mysterious, dotted with omissions and evasions, as Christopher Bush, who was born Charlie Christmas Bush on the day of the Nativity in 1885 in the Norfolk village of Great Hockham, to Charles Walter Bush and his second wife, Eva Margaret Long. While the father of Christopher Bush's Detection Club colleague and near exact contemporary Henry Wade (the pseudonym of Henry Lancelot Aubrey-Fletcher) was a baronet who lived in an elegant Georgian mansion and claimed extensive ownership of fertile English fields, Christopher's father resided in a cramped cottage and toiled in fields as a farm laborer, a term that in the late Victorian and Edwardian era, his son lamented many years afterward, "had in it something of contempt....There was something almost of serfdom about it."

Charles Walter Bush was a canny though mercurial individual, his only learning, his son recalled, having been "acquired at the Sunday school." A man of parts, Charles was a tenant farmer of three acres, a thatcher, bricklayer and carpenter (fittingly for the father of a detective novelist, coffins were his specialty), a village radical and a most adept poacher. After a flight from Great Hockham, possibly on account of his poaching activities, Charles, a widower with a baby son whom he had left in the care of his mother, resided in London, where he worked for a firm of spice importers. At a dance in the city, Charles met Christopher's mother, Eva Long, a lovely and sweet-natured young milliner and bonnet maker, sweeping her off her feet with a combination of "good looks and a certain plausibility." After their marriage the couple left London to live in a tiny rented cottage in Great Hockham, where Eva over the next eighteen years gave birth to three sons and five daughters and perforce learned the challenging ways of rural domestic economy.

Decades later an octogenarian Christopher Bush, in his memoir *Winter Harvest: A Norfolk Boyhood* (1967), characterized Great Hockham as a rustic rural redoubt where many of the words that fell from the tongues of the native inhabitants "were those of Shakespeare, Milton and the Authorised Version....Still in general use were words that were standard in Chaucer's time, but had since lost a certain respectability." Christopher amusingly recalled as a young boy telling his mother that a respectable neighbor woman had used profanity, explaining that in his hearing she had told her husband, "George, wipe you that shit off that pig's arse, do you'll datty your trousers," to which his mother had responded that although that particular usage of a four-letter word had not really been *swearing*, he was not to give vent to such language himself.

Great Hockham, which in Christopher Bush's youth had a population of about four hundred souls, was composed of a score or so of cottages, three public houses, a post-office, five shops, a couple of forges and a pair of churches, All Saint's and the Primitive Methodist Chapel, where the Bush family rather vocally worshipped. "The village lived by farming, and most of its men were labourers," Christopher recollected. "Most of the children left school as soon as the law permitted: boys to be absorbed somehow into the land and the girls to go into domestic service." There were three large farms and four smaller ones, and, in something of an anomaly, not one but two squires--the original squire, dubbed "Finch" by Christopher, having let the shooting rights at Little Hockham Hall to one "Green," a wealthy international banker, making the latter man a squire by courtesy. Finch owned most of the local houses and farms, in traditional form receiving rents for them personally on Michaelmas; and when Christopher's father fell out with Green, "a red-faced, pompous, blustering man," over a political election, he lost all of the banker's business, much to his mother's distress. Yet against all odds and adversities, Christopher's life greatly diverged from settled norms in Great Hockham, incidentally producing one of the most distinguished detective novelists from the Golden Age of detective fiction.

Although Christopher Bush was born in Great Hockham, he spent his earliest years in London living with his mother's much older sister, Elizabeth, and her husband, a fur dealer by the name of James Streeter, the couple having no children of their own. Almost certainly of illegitimate birth, Eva had been raised by the Long family from her infancy. She once told her youngest daughter how she recalled the Longs being visited, when she was a child, by a "fine lady in a carriage," whom she believed was her birth mother. Or is it possible that the "fine lady in a carriage" was simply an imaginary figment, like the aristocratic fantasies of Philippa Palfrey in P.D. James's *Innocent Blood* (1980), and that Eva's "sister" Elizabeth was in fact her mother?

The Streeters were a comfortably circumstanced couple at the time they took custody of Christopher. Their household included two maids and a governess for the young boy, whose doting but dutiful "Aunt Lizzie" devoted much of her time to the performance of "good works among the East End poor." When Christopher was seven years old, however, drastically straightened financial circumstances compelled the Streeters to leave London for Norfolk, by the way returning the boy to his birth parents in Great Hockham.

Fortunately the cause of the education of Christopher, who was not only a capable village cricketer but a precocious reader and scholar, was taken up both by his determined and devoted mother and an idealistic local elementary school headmaster. In his teens Christopher secured a scholarship to Norfolk's Thetford Grammar School, one of England's oldest educational institutions, where Thomas Paine had studied a century-and-a-half earlier. He left Thetford in 1904 to take a position as a junior schoolmaster, missing a chance to go to Cambridge University on yet another scholarship. (Later he proclaimed himself thankful for this turn of events, sardonically speculating that had he received a Cambridge degree he "might have become an exceedingly minor don or something as staid and static and respectable as a publisher.") Christopher would teach in English schools for the next twenty-seven years, retiring at the age of 46 in 1931, after he had established a successful career as a detective novelist.

Christopher's romantic relationships proved far rockier than his career path, not to mention every bit as murky as his mother's familial antecedents. In 1911, when Christopher was teaching in Wood Green School, a co-educational institution in Oxfordshire, he wed county council schoolteacher Ella Maria Pinner, a daughter of a baker neighbor of the Bushes in Great Hockham. The two appear never actually to have lived together, however, and in 1914, when Christopher at the age of 29 headed to war in the 16th (Public Schools) Battalion of the Middlesex Regiment, he falsely claimed in his attestation papers, under penalty of two years' imprisonment with hard labor, to be unmarried.

After four years of service in the Great War, including a year-long stint in Egypt, Christopher returned in 1919 to his position at Wood Green School, where he became involved in another romantic relationship, from which he soon desired to extricate himself. (A photo of the future author, taken at this time in Egypt, shows a rather dashing, thin-mustached man in uniform and is signed "Chris," suggesting that he had dispensed with "Charlie" and taken in its place a diminutive drawn from his middle name.) The next year Winifred Chart, a mathematics teacher at Wood Green, gave birth to a son, whom she named Geoffrey Bush. Christopher was the father of Geoffrey, who later in life became a noted English composer, though for reasons best known to himself Christopher never acknowledged his son. (A letter Geoffrey once sent him was returned unopened.) Winifred claimed that she and Christopher had married but separated, but she refused to speak of her purported spouse forever after and she destroyed all of his letters and other mementos, with the exception of a book of poetry that he had written for her

CHRISTOPHER BUSH

during what she termed their engagement.

Christopher's true mate in life, though with her he had no children, was Florence Marjorie Barclay, the daughter of a draper from Ballymena, Northern Ireland, and, like Ella Pinner and Winifred Chart, a schoolteacher. Christopher and Marjorie likely had become romantically involved by 1929, when Christopher dedicated to her his second detective novel, *The Perfect Murder Case*; and they lived together as man and wife from the 1930s until her death in 1968 (after which, probably not coincidentally, Christopher stopped publishing novels). Christopher returned with Marjorie to the vicinity of Great Hockham when his writing career took flight, purchasing two adjoining cottages and commissioning his father and a stepbrother to build an extension consisting of a kitchen, two bedrooms and a new staircase. (The now sprawling structure, which Christopher called "Home Cottage," is now a bed and breakfast grandiloquently dubbed "Home Hall.") After a falling-out with his father, presumably over the conduct of Christopher's personal life, he and Marjorie in 1932 moved to Beckley, Sussex, where they purchased Horsepen, a lovely Tudor plaster and timber-framed house. In 1953 the couple settled at their final home, The Great House, a centuries-old structure (now a boutique hotel) in Lavenham, Suffolk.

From these three houses Christopher maintained a lucrative and critically esteemed career as a novelist, publishing both detective novels as Christopher Bush and, commencing in 1933 with the acclaimed book *Return* (in the UK, *God and the Rabbit*, 1934), regional novels purposefully drawing on his own life experience, under the pen name Michael Home. (During the 1940s he also published espionage novels under the Michael Home pseudonym.) Although his first detective novel, *The Plumley Inheritance*, made a limited impact, with his second, *The Perfect Murder Case*, Christopher struck gold. The latter novel, a big seller in both the UK and the US, was published in the former country by the prestigious Heinemann, soon to become the publisher of the detective novels of Margery Allingham and Carter Dickson (John Dickson Carr), and in the latter country by the Crime Club imprint of Doubleday, Doran, one of the most important publishers of mystery fiction in the United States.

Over the decade of the 1930s Christopher Bush published, in both the UK and the US as well as other countries around the world, some of the finest detective fiction of the Golden Age, prompting the brilliant Thirties crime fiction reviewer, author and Oxford University Press editor Charles Williams to avow: "Mr. Bush writes of as thoroughly enjoyable murders as any I know." (More recently, mystery genre authority B.A. Pike dubbed these novels by Bush, whom he praised as "one of the most reliable and resourceful of true detective writers"; "Golden Age baroque, rendered remarkable by some extraordinary flights of fancy.") In 1937 Christopher Bush became, along with Nicholas Blake, E.C.R. Lorac and Newton Gayle (the writing team of Muna Lee and Maurice West Guinness), one of the final authors initiated into the Detection Club before the outbreak of the Second World War and with it the demise of the Golden Age. Afterward he continued publishing a detective novel or more a year, with his final book in 1968 reaching a total of 63, all of them detailing the investigative adventures of lanky and bespectacled gentleman amateur detective Ludovic Travers. Concurring as I do with the encomia of Charles Williams and B.A. Pike, I will end this introduction by thanking Avril MacArthur for providing invaluable biographical information on her great uncle, and simply wishing fans of classic crime fiction good times as they discover (or rediscover), with this latest splendid series of Dean Street Press classic crime fiction reissues, Christopher Bush's Ludovic Travers detective novels. May a new "Bush public" yet arise!

Curtis Evans

The Case of the Hanging Rope (1937)

CHRISTOPHER BUSH'S seventeenth Ludovic "Ludo" Travers detective novel, *The Case of the Hanging Rope* (*The Wedding Night Murder* in the US), concerns the murder of fictional glamorous celebrity British woman aviator (or aviatrix, as people tended to say in those days) Sonia Vorge. It was published in the UK in July 1937, the same month that real-life glamorous celebrity American woman aviator Amelia Earhart (1897-1937) tragically disappeared over the Pacific Ocean during the final quarter of her attempted flight around the world, which at 29,000 miles (47,000 km) had been intended to set the record as the longest global flight in history. Already world-renowned as the first woman ever to fly solo nonstop across the Atlantic Ocean (following in the path of Charles Lindbergh, who had preceded Earhart by five years, in 1927), Earhart in 1936 had begun planning the flight that ended, presumably, in her death and was much in trans-Atlantic news that year, the period when Christopher Bush was writing *The Case of the Hanging Rope*.

The internationally famous Earhart was far from the only prominent woman pilot of her day, however. Another such individual who would surely have been well-known to Christopher Bush was the glamorous Englishwoman Amy Johnson (1903-1941), who, among other accomplishments, set the solo speed record for the flight from London to Cape Town, South Africa; was the first woman to fly solo from England to Australia; and, with her co-pilot, the first person to fly in one day from London to Moscow. Like Earhart, Johnson suffered a mysterious--and to this day much debated--death during a flight. Although Christopher Bush's Sonia Vorge, who is doomed to die a violent death in *The Case of the Hanging Rope*, has many of the qualities of such daring Thirties women as Amelia Earhart and Amy Johnson, she is an altogether dark figment of the author's imagination, up until her frankly deserved demise behaving as what in American crime fiction would be termed a femme fatale:

a conscienceless destroyer of unfortunate individuals, male and female, ensnared by the lure of her deadly attractions.

On the death of her parents (a naturalized Russian father and an English mother--the latter one of the Carne family), explains Bush of notorious Sonia Vorge, "she had come into a fortune of something like forty thousand [pounds], and had been a headliner from then on":

> The cheap press always spoke of her as exotic, mysterious and glamorous; not too far-fetched, perhaps, for an ivory complexion, almond eyes, red lips, and black hair cropped close except for a straight fringe that ran above the line of eyebrow. Then there was her dress, which was as exotic as herself—wide silk trousers gathered in at the ankles, blouse with buttoned front and high collar, and a kind of turban swathing for head-dress; the whole giving an effect which was usually described as Cossack.
>
> Then there were the men with whose names she was from time to time connected—a pianist of world repute, a famous film-star, an ex-Crown Prince, Maurice Trove himself, and, of course, Sidley Cordovan. . . .

Prominent theatrical producer Sidley Cordovan had broken off his engagement with Sonia, to the world "saying some pretty hard things" about his former fiancée, after which a quickly rebounding Sonia took with her as co-pilot aviator Maurice Trove (son of art dealer Sir Raphael Breye's business partner), with whom she had earlier flown across the Atlantic, on a "mad winter flight" from the Riviera to the Soviet Union and back. Sonia crashed her plane in the Austrian Alps, whereupon she left Maurice to suffer, presumably, a ghastly frozen death. This was not the first time someone riding in a machine with Sonia had met with an untimely end. There was also that tragic case of Sonia's distant relative Irene Carne—the daughter of portrait painter Wilfred Carne and his wife Henrietta, a sister of Sir Raphael Breye; a cousin of Sidley Cordovan; and the sister of Philip Carne, playwright and poet, and Patrick Carne, contract-bridge expert. Irene was with her kinswoman in an Alpine race (Sonia had taken up competitive auto racing at the age of eighteen) when Sonia crashed her car, killing Irene while herself escaping with comparatively minor injuries.

Now, in the oddest turn yet, a suddenly reconciled Sonia and Sidley have married at a London registry office, with Ludovic Travers, a friend and social acquaintance of the various parties, on hand as one of the witnesses. At the wedding Sonia impulsively invites Ludo to have lunch with her the next day, promising him: "You shall not be bored." However, Sonia never makes it to her lunch date with Ludo, for around midnight on the evening of her wedding she is stabbed to death at her and Sidley's honeymoon suite at Montage Court, the reputedly haunted former residence of Sir Raphael Braye (who has left England for France, where, in his dotage, he lives a reclusive life with his famous art collection.) In an adjoining room Sidley is found lying on his bed in a stupor, while a noose hangs grimly from a nearby beam. Travers scoff at the notion of Coales, the superstitious butler at Montage Court, that a baneful ghost lurked in the suite that fatal night, but beyond question something hellish happened on Sonia and Sidley's honeymoon. Had self-centered Sonia's sinful past finally caught up with her?

Happily, Christopher Bush provided a family tree of Breyes and Carnes (with sidelights on Sonia Vorge and Maurice Trove), in this, one of his most involved mystery stories yet. The plot of *The Case of the Hanging Rope* concerns complicated relationships within a family of eccentric artists and intellectuals and gives more of a place to female characters. It recalls much of the work of Crime Queen Margery Allingham in the Thirties and Forties and signifies a continued movement in Bush's late Thirties work toward the manners mystery of Allingham and her sister Crime Queens Dorothy L. Sayers and Ngaio Marsh, a trio who were having a profound impact on British mystery writing at this time--though near the end of this weird and witty brainteaser there is, presumably for the old boys, just a spot of "Bull-dog Drummond stuff," as Travers puts it to a pal.

TO THE READER

IT IS BEWILDERING and irritating to meet in the first chapter of a book such an array of presumably vital characters that many more chapters must be read before the mind retains and localizes them. In the chapter that follows, any such bewilderment and irritation will be avoided if the reader will spend no more than two minutes on the family tree of the Breyes which contains every important character. These are all imaginary and have no reference to any living person. Figures in parentheses give the age in 1937, and the absence of such figures indicates that the character is dead.

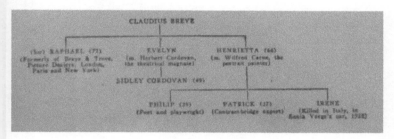

Of the remaining characters, SONIA VORGE (27) was a distant relation of Henrietta Carne, while MAURICE TROVE (38?), the airman, was the son of SIR RAPHAEL's partner in the firm of Breye and Trove. It is assumed, presumptuously perhaps, that both LUDOVIC TRAVERS and SUPERINTENDENT WHARTON are already known.

I
PORTENTS

ONE MONDAY EVENING of late April, two days before the wedding of Sonia Vorge and Sidley Cordovan, Travers was in the small reading room of the Sophocles Club in Mantford Street. His back was to the door and he was consulting a volume of old playbills in connection with a new book he was contemplating—a species of successor to his first venture in literary criminology, *Kensington Gore*. But whereas that particular book had dealt with the murders that had from time to time, and more or less happily, eliminated blue-bloods and highbrows, the new work was to deal with those killings which had concerned, with no small irony, the stage itself: tragedies, in fact, that had eliminated the tragedians. There had been three people at least in the room, and then all at once he was aware that there was no more than one, and that from the direction of that one person was coming the queerest of sounds. So he hooked off his horn-rims and polished them—a trick of his when at a mental loss or on the edge of discovery—and craned his neck round. At the dim distance across the room the man was unknown to him, though another queer thing was that his horn-rims were huge as Travers's own. As for the sounds, they were merely a snoring, yet something in its way unique, for it came as regularly with the outward breathing of the sleeper as the tick of a clock. It was sonorous and yet muffled, with a hint of strangulation, and was possessed, so Travers whimsically assured himself, of a nuisance value of which its producer ought to be made aware.

But as he finished his volume and replaced it in its cupboard, there was a tap at the door and a steward came in with the evening papers. He also switched on another light, whereat two things happened: the sleeper awoke, and Travers knew him for Philip Carne. Travers's head went round quickly again, for of all people he wanted to meet, Carne was the last. There was something repulsive about the man which Travers would have found it hard to define. Carne, poet and playwright, was clever—there was no doubt whatever about that—and if compared with the poetic bulk, whether of the introspective school or the whimsies or the good old back-to-nature (so apt for the radio on a Sunday afternoon), he seemed in a class by himself.

But Travers had always felt a something frightening about those bitter social satires of Philip Carne, and that vast capacity for hate. As for his plays—published, but rarely performed—they were generally Renaissance in period; of a school that outdid Ford and Webster; voluptuous, passionate and intricately indecent. Sidley Cordovan, when once asked why he produced no play of Philip Carne's, hit a nail shrewdly on the head. "I don't want my pornography acted," he said. "I buy mine in little paper-covered books, smuggled over from France."

But curiosity, or what Ludovic Travers himself would have called an interest in his fellow man, caused a new craning round, and there was Carne staring intently at the front page of the *Evening Record*. Then those monstrous horn-rims began to fascinate Travers. He had been aware but vaguely that Carne wore glasses at all, and now the droll play of the electric light on Carne's lenses gave to his face a quaint bellicose air, far different from its usual bored superciliousness and over-consciousness of brains and breeding.

Then Travers was aware of something else, that the front page of the paper had something which Carne was finding extremely disturbing, for he was frowning at it and shaking his head, though the light so flickered on his lenses that Travers could not see his eyes. Then suddenly he looked up and gave a little start.

"It's Travers, isn't it?"

"In person," Travers assured him gravely.

"In person?" Carne found the answer strange.

There are those in clubs and elsewhere who, by those endless silences which are a tradition in keeping with the old school tie, have achieved a reputation for profound and inscrutable wisdom. But Travers, by his own loquacity, would tempt some tiling of that loquacity from others, with the hope of striking some rich lode for professional profit.

"That's right," he said, and was at once tickled at the idea. "To you, as an eminent playwright, I say that I'm here in person. To a doctor I might have said I was still in the land of the living." He waved a hand. "A theme, one might say, on which to extemporize."

Carne ignored the babbling, and with a slight raising of eyebrows handed over the paper.

"What do you think of that?"

There was little need to read, for the news was something in the nature of a shriek. IS MAURICE TROVE STILL ALIVE? was the clamant headline, and flanking the letter-press was yet another photograph of Sonia Vorge. Travers scanned a line or two then peered across.

"Preposterous, surely! There wasn't any doubt about his being dead."

"I don't know," Carne said. "I don't think we've a right to go as far as that. Sonia might have panicked and lost her head." His thin lips drooped. "I was one of the few people rather suspicious at the time."

Travers shook his head. "The whole thing was madness. Flying from the Riviera across the Alps to Moscow and back, the lord knows why. But I don't agree that she panicked. You can hardly imagine Sonia Vorge doing that. The plane crashed in the Austrian Alps on the return journey, if I remember rightly, and Trove had his legs damaged so she went for help. She would have died herself if she hadn't stumbled by sheer blind, blazing luck on that forester, and that was two days later, so how Trove could have lived is past my imagining." He paused at Carne's chair on his way to the door. "My own idea is that the whole thing's a cheap effort at publicity in view of Sonia's wedding."

"You may be right," Carne told him languidly. "But you'll notice they say they've had the reliable evidence of a man who claimed to have seen Trove in Odessa three weeks ago. Odessa is in Russia after all, you know, and it's three months since the crash, so Trove might have been picked up and got over his hurt."

Travers smiled dryly. "Anonymity and truth were never blood brothers. Besides, if Trove is alive, why didn't he tell the world so from Odessa? And how'd he get to Odessa from Austria?"

"He may have had reasons of his own," Carne said. "He may even have lost his memory."

"Ah, you dramatists!" said Travers roguishly. "Well, I must be pushing off. My very kindest wishes to your mother when you see her."

"That will be in an hour," Carne said. "I'm staying at Severns for a day or two."

"Working?"

Carne shrugged his shoulders. "Merely a Grand Guignol trifle for the B.B.C." He looked up. "Did I hear you'd be at the wedding?"

There had been a veiled irony in the question. Travers smiled gently.

"Well yes. Cordovan and I happened to be doing a deal together and he said something about acting as witness." The smile became most friendly. "Naturally I had to accept. A little publicity's not to be sneezed at."

Carne grunted. "A lot of publicity you need! It's wealthy amateurs like you who queer the whole pitch."

"Splendid!" said Travers. "Then you must put me in one of your next poems—or do you call them castigations?"

But once more Carne was ignoring the babble. He had picked up the newspaper again and was gazing sneeringly at that front page.

"What I'm wondering at the moment is what Sonia will think when she reads this." Then he stared. "Hallo! Listen to this in the Stop Press:

Re Maurice Trove rumours, Sonia Vorge, in answer to our interviewer, said she had nothing to modify in her original story. See later editions.

A bit fishy, don't you think?"

"I'm not interested," Travers said, and looked down for a moment at Carne, who had taken off the horn-rims and was leaning languidly back as if to rest his eyes. "I didn't know, by the way, that you'd taken to glasses?"

"Worn them for months," he said, and hooked them on again. "I'd be as blind as a bat without them. And all on account of that bad time I had last year." He looked up. "By the way, you can tell me something. Is it a fact that a good many people's eyes go wrong at forty?"

"Yes," Travers said. "I believe that's a fact. I must admit that my own remain pretty constant." He moved off again towards the door. "But, talking about nothing in particular, are you aware that you have a most devastating snore?"

Carne gave him a quick look, then shook a sheepish head.

"Asleep, was I? Sorry, but I've been told about that once or twice recently. My mother has mentioned it." He shook his head again, and dolefully. "Something to do with my nose, I believe. They tell me a trifling operation would put it right."

As Ludovic Travers strolled towards his flat at St. Martin's Chambers, he was still thinking about Philip Carne and trying to analyse that hostility towards both Cordovan and Sonia Vorge. Every reason, of course, why Carne should hate Sidley Cordovan, who had sneered at those literary plays of his and spoken of the Grand Guignol efforts as the products of a diseased mind. But Sonia was different. Surely somewhere recently he had heard Carne's name and Sonia's coupled? Where was it?—and then he remembered.

A man at the club, it had been, talking to a friend, with Travers a kind of off-hand third.

"By the way I ran across Philip Carne yesterday, and who do you think he was with? Sonia Vorge! In a little tea-place in Chelsea, talking away with their heads together. I think I rather spoiled things because they slipped out a minute or so later."

That had been the talk and it had given the impression of a clandestine meeting and a very definite understanding. Old Henrietta Carne might never have forgiven Sonia but that was no reason why Philip should be bitter or hostile. And then Travers tried to work out dates in his mind. When had that Chelsea meeting taken place? The crash had been in January;

Sonia had got back to England in middle February. Yes—and Travers nodded to himself—it had been before the announcement of Sonia's re-engagement to Sidley Cordovan. There then was the explanation of Carne's various sneers. That re-engagement of Sonia's had knocked him clean off his perch, and no wonder he was bitter if she were marrying Sidley.

Then a line of splash bills caught Travers's eye, and again he was nodding to himself:

SONIA'S WEDDING—LATEST
MAURICE TROVE SENSATION!
SONIA'S HELICOPTER?

Still front-page news, was Sonia Vorge. Her father was a naturalized Russian and her mother English, and a Carne, and on the tragic death of her parents she had come into a fortune of something like forty thousand, and had been a head-liner from then on. For one thing she was a beauty, and an uncommon one. The cheap press always spoke of her as exotic, mysterious and glamorous; not too far-fetched perhaps for an ivory complexion, almond eyes, red lips, and black hair cropped close except for a straight fringe that ran above the line of eyebrow. Then there was her dress, which was as exotic as herself—wide silk trousers gathered in at the ankles, blouse with buttoned front and high collar, and a kind of turban swathing for head-dress; the whole giving an effect which was usually described as Cossack.

Then there were the men with whose names she was from time to time connected—a pianist of world repute, a famous film star, an ex-Crown Prince, Maurice Trove himself, and, of course, Sidley Cordovan. There had been the sensation when Cordovan broke off the engagement—with some pretty hard words, as rumour had it—when she decided to take Trove as co-pilot for the mad winter flight across the Alps to Russia and back. Greater still had been the sensation when in March the re-engagement had been announced; and with the publication of the date, hour and place of the wedding, the excitement had increased, with a good few still betting that Sonia was the last person in the world to tie herself down in marriage.

As for her various exploits, she was driving racing cars at eighteen and picking up prizes at Brooklands. Then Brooklands proved too tame and at nineteen she was competing in the continental circuits and holding her own against men. Then came that terrible affair in the Alpine race when Irene Carne was her passenger. Irene, always a worshiper of Sonia, was studying music in Rome, and Henrietta was not even aware that she was to accompany Sonia in that race, so no wonder the news of Irene's death in the wreck had come as an overwhelming shock.

Sonia escaped with a broken arm and smashed ribs, and in the autumn, as if to show that her nerve was still good, competed in, and carried off, the big Turin event, with an exhibition of dare-devil, hair-raising driving in lashing rain that scared a good few from the starting post. After that Sonia took up parachuting and gliding, and finally long-distance flying. The then Cape Town to London record was broken by a day, and the return by hours. Then came the two Atlantic flights, in the second of which Maurice Trove was co-pilot, and so to that Russian flight and its tragic ending for Trove.

Palmer, Travers's man, gave an interesting sidelight on Sonia as front-page news. As soon as Travers got in he produced the evening papers and gave that quaint little incipient bow of his. Though he had the look of an archdeacon, and had valeted old Colonel Travers and had known the infant Ludovic in his first pram, he was more than punctilious about taking the mere suggestion of a liberty. "Interesting news about Miss Vorge, if I may say so, sir. Very remarkable if Captain Trove should still be alive, sir."

"Yes," said Travers, and ran his eye over the front pages of the other two papers. "What's your own idea of Sonia Vorge, by the way?"

"My idea, sir? Well, she's a remarkably handsome woman, sir. A real beauty, as they say, sir."

Travers nodded. "I think you're right. I think if she cared two hoots for such things she could be even more—well, beautiful."

Palmer nodded comprehendingly. "You mean the way she dresses, sir. But a very brave woman, sir. Absolutely reckless, you might say." He shook his head. "A lot of people say, sir, it's a kind of showing-off."

Travers smiled as his mind's eye saw Sonia, chin cupped in hands and face wearing that look of aloof and almost supercilious self-possession.

"I don't agree with you there. I don't think she troubles a button about outside opinion. She's made up her mind to live life her own way, and that's all there is to it."

"Heartless, I think they call her, sir." Palmer was a great reader of the Sunday key-hole press. "But about that helicopter, sir. Do you think it's true?"

"I don't know," Travers said. "You tell me about it."

The wedding was to be at Hengate Register Office at two o'clock, and behind that Office lies an open space of ground in possession of the Hengate Council. According to the *Evening Searchlight*, a helicopter was to be waiting there for the couple after the ceremony, and the honeymoon was to be spent in Egypt, where Sidley Cordovan was to collect material for his big autumn production at the *Auriole*.

"I know nothing about it," Travers said, and smiled to himself at the thought of Sidley's pink bulk wedged in the rear seat. "Between ourselves I had the idea they might be going to St. Peranne. Old Sir Raphael's villa is right above the bay there, and I believe she flies there occasionally. If I remember rightly it was from there she started on that last flight of hers to Russia."

"But he's a kind of hermit, sir," Palmer said.

"Sir Raphael?" He smiled. "A man's got the right to shut himself up with his pictures. Personally, if I'd met as many queer clients as he has in his time, I'd take thundering good care to retire to where I'd never be pestered."

"Yes," said Palmer, and nodded reminiscently. "I remember in your father's time, sir, how people used to speak of the brilliant Breyes. A queer family, sir, if I may say so." He gave his little bow. "Now if you'll pardon me, sir, I must get back to the kitchen. Dinner in fifteen minutes, sir."

While Travers prepared himself for his evening meal he was thinking over that remark that Palmer had made about the brilliant Breyes. Brilliant was the word, with its hint of the ephemeral. Raphael, the greatest expert of his age, throwing up everything after his partner's death and taking that vast collection of his to a villa in the South of France. Some queer kink or insanity there had always been about Raphael Breye, and now he was probably dying from the top, like Swift's oak.

Then there had been Evelyn, the greatest tragic actress of her time, and what she had made of Herbert Cordovan. Those two had ruled the theatrical roost, and both had gone out like candles in the wind. He could still recall the horror he had felt when Evelyn's reason had given way, and the hushing-up there had been after the public breakdown. Then Cordovan had died within the year and Sidley had taken over everything. Sidley— nothing much abnormal about him; shrimp-faced and blue-eyed, and with the air of a plump country squire, but rarely making a mistake and gifted with so many lucky intuitions as to be in no need of brains.

Then there was Henrietta, the Edwardian hostess, making the most of that little charlatan of a Wilfred Carne. For years he had been the most fashionable portrait-painter of his time, and then his bubble too had burst. Some said he had left never a penny when he died, and everyone knew Henrietta was a pensioner of Raphael. But there was nothing abnormal about Henrietta, save a singular sanity. Crippled with rheumatism as she was, she could still hold to the grand manner. No whining or complaining from Henrietta. Her look was still as imperious and her voice as tart as when Travers had first met her, a year before her husband's death, when he himself was still at Cambridge. She had overawed him then and she could still rather terrify him now.

Irene would have been like her, had she lived, unless that musical talent of hers had amounted to something of genius and she had gone the brilliant way of the others. As for Philip, the mind itself became almost furtive in assessing him. Good-looking he might be in an Irving kind of way, and—when he was so minded—as charmingly delightful in manner as Travers himself; and yet one felt the calculation and knew the charm for background and drapery and wondered what lay in the real mind. And it was a tortuous, distorted mind, full of private grievances and nourished hates, that had their own queer workings-out.

And as for the last of the Breyes—Patrick—the abnormality about him was that he should be subnormal, for a Breye. Some said he was the finest poker-player in Europe, which was probably true, for no man looked less like the part. Everything about him was unobtrusive: his nods, his smiles, his quiet monosyllabic remarks, and his gentle eyes. Correct but colourless—that was Patrick Carne; with the look of a well-bred sheep and yet making enough out of contract bridge to keep himself in that flat of his at the back of Sloane Square, and to keep up appearances at his clubs.

Travers sat down to his meal and as Palmer came in with the soup, the phone rang. Travers took the call himself, and as soon as he heard the voice he was smiling.

"Why, certainly! Any time you like. Why not nip in and have a bite with me now? . . . You will? Splendid! . . . Five minutes, then. Cheerio, George."

He turned to Palmer. "Take the soup away again, will you? Superintendent Wharton's coming in for a few minutes. Just fix up the extra meal, if you don't mind."

Palmer had nodded in a gratified way at the mention of George Wharton's name, for the Superintendent was something of an old friend. But Travers was frowning to himself at the queer appositeness of George Wharton's opening words, for Wharton had begun with: "You're a pretty close acquaintance of Sonia Vorge, aren't you?"

Then in his quick secretive way he had hurried on to the request for a minute or two of Travers's time, and had added that he was ringing up from the Stanfield Hotel, though what that had to do with everything Travers was unable to fathom. But it was certainly like George to be mysterious, if only for the purpose of producing the rabbit at the right time from the hat.

II
WEDDING EVE

THROUGHOUT his career George Wharton had profited much from the fact that he bore little resemblance to the accepted type—the type, for instance, which included Chief-Inspector Norris, his right-hand man. Norris would have been taken for a policeman in his gardening clothes, for there was no getting away from that ramrod spine of his, and the set of his head as if he had never forgotten the days when he wore a helmet. But George Wharton had the air of a none too prosperous clerk, and when he put on his antiquated spectacles and pursed out his lips beneath the weeping-willow of a moustache, he was the perfect paterfamilias, the least bit downtrodden and decidedly harassed.

The first thing he announced that night when he entered Travers's flat was that he had no more than twenty minutes to spare. Travers was pouring him out a sherry.

"Don't say it accusingly, George," he said. "It isn't my fault if you propose to gulp your meal."

Wharton gave a grunt in his best manner. Travers drew him in a chair, for the soup was coming in.

"Now what's all the trouble? And why the question about Sonia Vorge?"

Wharton tucked the napkin well inside his collar and took a taste or two of the soup before he spoke.

"Did you read that hint in the *Record*, that Maurice Trove might be alive?"

Travers admitted an acquaintance with the barest outlines.

"I'll tell you just what happened," Wharton said. "At about half-past four this afternoon a man rang up the *Record* and said he had some news that might interest them. He gave his name as Doctor Stavangel, and referred them to the vice-consul at Constantinople—or Istanbul, or whatever you call it—for his bona-fides. All the same, he said, he didn't want his name divulged, and I might also add that he appeared to be speaking in a very agitated voice. His news was that he had seen Maurice Trove in Odessa, beyond a shadow of a doubt. He said he had seen Trove and hailed him, and that as soon as Trove caught sight of him he nipped inside a door and vanished; you know, bolting out of his way. Stavangel said he knew Trove well, having served at the same air station in France the last year of the war."

Travers raised his eyebrows. "And where do you come in?"

"All in good time," Wharton said, and swished that huge moustache of his with the napkin. The second course was on the table before he resumed.

"I know Palmer's to be trusted," he said, "but I'd just as soon keep this strictly confidential. What happened then was that the *Record* decided to print something, and Stavangel was asked to arrange a confidential interview forthwith, and they'd send a man round. He agreed, but the interviewer was to be there at five o'clock sharp, and he was to come in by the side door—you know the Stanfield Hotel?—and go right up to room 143. Stavangel was most agitated and emphatic about all that. So the *Record* sent along Dustin, one of their star men. Now I'll do the story from the hotel angle."

Beer was his favourite tipple and he filled his glass. Another wipe of the moustache and, between bites, he was off again.

"Stavangel was a man of about fifty, of medium height and wearing a black beard of the untidy sort. The clerk recalled two things about him when he registered—that he kept looking round in a highly suspicious way, and that he had a scar which ran from the back of his right hand down along his wrist. Stavangel had a bag with him and after he had phoned he said he was fetching the balance of his luggage at once. He was then believed to have left the hotel but it can't be proved, and if he came back, then no one saw him."

Travers nodded, and waited.

"Now for the jiggery-pokery," said Wharton. "Dustin was outside the door of 143 well on time and was just going to tap when he noticed the door was slightly ajar. So he took a peep inside, and all he saw was that someone had been playing the devil inside the room. Stavangel had left that small bag of his behind him and it'd been slit open and everything scattered over the floor—odd clothing, pair of shoes, an empty wallet, and three books dealing with oil and the Middle East. Whoever had done it had also hunted through the drawers of the chest and the wardrobe, and turned over the bedclothes. On the dressing-table was a half-sheet of writing-paper, pretty good in quality, and on the back of it a slight smear of what's probably blood. On it was printed this."

Travers polished his glasses and had a look while Palmer saw to the sweet course. Wharton gazed abstractedly at the ceiling.

damlp sfgty ldyks olgtu cavxm jifhm wihlx ipodf vndur

That was the lettering, and so obviously a code that after the first glance Travers was staring somewhat blankly at it.

"Keep it if you like," Wharton said. "I made a couple of copies. The original had some excellent prints on it, by the way."

"Queer sort of happening," Travers said. "And this chap Stavangel's never turned up?"

Wharton gave an elaborate shrug of the shoulders.

"And you've found nothing out about him at all?"

"Not a thing. The clothes were well worn and had no marks. The books were fairly old and had nothing but his name. The empty wallet was a perfectly ordinary type. In fact, we don't know a thing, and we haven't been able so far to find out a thing. As far as we're concerned, he's vanished, as they say, into thin air." He waved an airy hand. "I'm not greatly concerned myself. Two of my men are on it and it happened to be in my district." His look took on a pert enquiry. "I shouldn't be surprised if it turns out to be a job for the Special Branch."

"As soon as you've gone into those bona-fides, you'll know more," Travers said. "All the same, George, there's something that tells me everything isn't quite what it seems. I always have a suspicion of men with beards."

"Oh?" said Wharton. "And what's your idea then?"

Travers smiled. "Don't round on me like that, George. All I'm saying is that I'd have liked things better if Stavangel hadn't had a beard." He gave a shrewd look. "I put it to you, and very tentatively. In view of the enormous publicity attached at this moment to Sonia Vorge, why shouldn't the *Record* have faked the whole affair?"

"No reason whatever," Wharton told him dryly, "except that they didn't. I have their implicit assurances to that effect, and their further assurances that if anyone is so foolish as to suggest such a thing, he's in for a first-class libel action." He gave another queer look. "Trove was a pretty good-looking chap, wasn't he?"

"Never saw him in my life," Travers said. "I've always heard he was a damn good sort, and most likeable."

"Would it make any difference to Sonia Vorge if he were alive?"

Travers stared at that question. Wharton was pushing his plate unconcernedly aside and making as if to rise from the table.

"That's a queer question, George," he said. "In what way do you ask it? Officially, or by way of gossip?"

"What do you mean?" said Wharton virtuously. Then he began filling his pipe and glancing rather pointedly at the clock. "Still, if you don't know, I reckon I'd better be on the move. Thanking you for an excellent meal."

Travers laughed. George's little subterfuges and trifles of showmanship had long become the obvious.

"Well, if only to have the pleasure of your company a minute or two longer, I'll answer your question. But I'd like you to take me seriously, because, you see, I may get an answer to some things I'd rather like to know myself. The answer to your question as to whether or not Trove's return might make a difference to Sonia, depends on certain things."

"Such as?"

"Well, if Sonia told any lies about that aeroplane crash, or forced landing or whatever it was, then Trove's return might be something in the nature of a showing-up. Then again, if Trove and she were in love with one another—though, frankly, I can't imagine her as being in love with anyone—then Trove's return might put a spoke in Wednesday's wedding."

"You know her fairly well?"

"I've met her exactly three times," Travers said. "The first was at Severns, the year Irene Carne was killed. Sonia regarded Henrietta Carne as a kind of aunt in those days."

"And where's this place Severns?"

"Not so far from Sevenoaks," Travers said. "Henrietta Carne has lived there since her husband's death and it was generally supposed that her brother—Sir Raphael, of course—bought it for her. It's only about ten miles from Montage Court, where he once used to house his collection."

Wharton grunted. "And about Sonia Vorge. Is there any truth in the idea that she's got as much feeling as a fish and is—well, cold-blooded and unscrupulous?"

Behind the melodrama of the question, Travers felt an earnestness.

"I can't tell you, George," he said. "I can give you my private opinion, for what it's worth."

"Good! Let's hear it."

"Well"—he frowned—"I don't think it's going to make sense to you, but I see Sonia as a member of what we might call the Breye set or clan. That means I see her as something abnormal and not too pleasant. She's just as big an egomaniac as Philip Carne but in a different way, because I honestly think she hates publicity. I believe that everything she's done, she's done for the sake of doing it—not for sensationalism. I don't think she has a farthing's worth of affection for any soul on earth. I believe that only once has she been what you might call moved."

"When that friend got killed in her car?"

"Lord, no!" Travers said. "If you remember—but you wouldn't though. You didn't know the facts. But I know she never wrote Henrietta a line, and in her statement to the press she merely said that Irene Carne wanted to be the passenger, and was a free agent, and that she herself took the same risks." He shook his head. "The only time in her life when Sonia Vorge was really touched on the raw was when Sidley Cordovan threw her over."

"Then why's she marrying him?"

Travers hooked off his glasses and began polishing them.

"Didn't I tell you there were things I wanted to find out for myself? I don't know why she's marrying him, unless . . ."

"Unless what?"

"Well"—he smiled grimly—"I'll answer another question of yours about whether or not she's unscrupulous. I know for a fact that the yarns aren't true that Sidley saved her from bankruptcy. She's run through the very devil of a pile, and where she gets her money from now I don't know, but it isn't from Sidley. In other words—and laugh if you like—I can conceive of no other reason why she's marrying him except to make his life hell."

Wharton peered over the tops of his glasses. "Putting him through it as a kind of revenge, is that it? But why shouldn't she have an eye on his money?"

Travers smiled dryly. "Ever buy a dozen oysters with the hope of finding a pearl? Sidley's the close-fisted kind."

"But he's mad on marrying her?"

"Only too obviously. She's a remarkably attractive woman for most men. Personally I'd rather get chained up to a she-leopard."

"Ah, well," said Wharton piously. "It takes all sorts to make a world." Out went his hand. "Much obliged for the meal and the information. Oh, before I forget it. I was to tell you from Jane that she supposed there wasn't a chance of your getting her a comfortable place to see the wedding couple?"

Travers saw Jane Wharton in his mind's eye, and smiled affectionately.

"So she's a Sonia fan, is she, George? Nothing doing, though. Between ourselves I expect several rubber-necked thousands have made a date for two o'clock on Wednesday. I've even decided it'll be too risky to go in my own car."

And on that Wednesday afternoon, Travers's prophecy proved only too true. A throng of women surged with him from the Tube station, and within a hundred yards of the Register Office the streets were hopelessly blocked and lines of police were fighting to clear something of a way. So Travers sheered towards the back, and there mounted police were keeping a clear passage before two cars that stood by the side door. Politeness availed him nothing; the surging mass swept him back and it was almost two o'clock when at last he induced two mounted police to believe his tale and force a way through to that side door.

In the office there was nothing but a suave decorum, so that Travers might have regarded those noises of the outside thousands as nothing but hallucination. A black-coated man sat at the usual desk, and the usual clerk flanked him. Patrick Carne gave the merest nod of greeting and his lips almost smiled. Sonia, in that modern, cold, metallic voice of hers, said evenly, "Here you are, then." Sidley alone was fussy, his shrimp-pink face wreathed with a smile and his lower chin bulging out above the dazzling white open collar.

"Sorry," Travers said. "Hope I haven't kept you all waiting."

"Poor darling," Sonia said. "You've torn your coat."

"Good lord!" said Travers, and grinned ruefully at where the lapel had been ripped. Patrick Carne watched mildly, as if afraid of being too interested, and then Sidley began clearing his throat.

"It's gone two . . . don't you think?"

The remark was general and apparently the Registrar did think, for he rose to begin the first formalities. Travers remained politely in the rear with Patrick Carne, than whom no one could have been less interested. Sonia might have been watching her trunk examined by the Customs, for she had the bored look of a person who has nothing whatever to declare, and the mild amusement of one who notes the fussiness of others.

Travers had never seen her looking so superb. That romantic costume had been discarded for the occasion and she was wearing a black kind of dress edged with red that went perfectly with the faint cream of her skin and the scarlet of her mouth. Her hat was a toque of fur, while the short fur coat looked as if it had cost Sidley or herself a pretty steep figure. Sidley was overdressed as usual, with a quite unnecessary white edging to the waistcoat of his lounge suit; linen just too stiff and immaculate, and spats a shade too light. He was nervous too, and kept rubbing his podgy hands together and snapping his eyes.

The Registrar's voice was droning on and Travers, as a gesture to a ceremony that at least would turn two into one, was slightly bending his head and casting only surreptitious glances around him. Quite the usual sort of place, he supposed, with a slight smell of mustiness, and a pretentious array of filing cabinets and lockers. Rather like a lawyer's office, in a way. Then he took a sideways squint at Patrick Carne. Curious how everything about him lacked a personal touch. His height was medium, for instance; his face well-bred enough but just ordinary; his hair and eyes an indeterminate brown, that most usual of colours; and even his suit a navy-blue, the very acme of convention.

"May I offer my congratulations?"

Travers came to himself with a start and realized that the ceremony was over. The Registrar was shaking hands and in a couple of minutes there was a sudden, stilted quiet such as comes on a station platform when the train has moved and then changed its mind. Travers boldly filled the breach.

"Well, well, well! So you're really married."

Sonia's voice followed coldly. "See to the cars, Sidley, will you?"

"Yes, yes," he said; hesitated, and then moved off towards the passage.

"We have Sidley's man and my maid parked here in that room," she explained. "Those cars outside are a blind."

"But how clever!" Travers said. "They go off in the cars and everyone will think it's you two. Whose was the bright idea?"

She shrugged her shoulders. "Sidley's, I believe. Probably at second hand." Then she was turning to Carne. "Be a darling, Patrick, and be sure they put up the umbrella to hide their faces. Sidley will never remember."

The two stood silent for a minute and then all at once there was a roar from outside that almost shattered the office windows. Through the window top could be seen a lorry, with a photographer turning his handle, and then there was another, and always that long steady roar.

"It seems to have gone off well," Travers said.

She gave no sign that she had heard and it was rather as if she were listening for something that had not yet come. Then suddenly her gloved hand was on his arm, and she was whispering.

"Lunch with me tomorrow. At my flat."

He stared.

"At one o'clock." There was a faint smile that seemed to have some bitter irony. "I promise you will not be bored."

The passage door was opening and again she was standing motionless and as if listening.

"Gone off first-rate," Sidley said. "They're chasing those cars still." He seemed suddenly aware of some queerness in the silence, and gave a little titter. "Two or three minutes and we might be moving . . . don't you think?"

"Where are you bound for?" Travers asked.

"Well"—he gave a quick look at Sonia—"at the moment I'm not allowed to say."

"Be looking out for the car, will you?" Sonia said quietly. Her hand went out to Patrick Carne. "Thank you so much, Patrick darling. I do hope your mother won't be too annoyed. And thank you too, Ludo." She smiled provocatively. "Heaven knows when I shall see you again."

Before Travers could find words she was moving to the door. The two men followed at a discreet distance and were just in time to see the quick rush for the car. Two minutes later they were walking through streets comparatively clear. Travers was taking the Tube back to town but Carne was going the opposite way.

"You don't happen to know where that honeymoon's being spent, I suppose?" Travers asked him.

"Never a notion," Carne said.

"Anything in that Egypt rumour?"

"No idea."

On they went, Travers shortening his strides to fit in with Carne's medium ones. Then all at once he grunted. "Queer, bloodless sort of business, don't you think? Or are Register Office marriages always like that? Sort of will you or won't you;

sign on the dotted line; heaven bless you, and here's your receipt. Seems a frightful waste of time you and me coming all this
way to witness a synopsis."

"Rather a bore," Carne said mildly. He halted and gave a little farewell nod. "Well, I'm going this way."

Carne stepped into the road. Two steps, and all at once there
was the hoot of a horn, the roar of a voice and the grind of brakes.
Travers's heart missed a beat, but Carne must have moved like
lightning for he seemed to leap sideways like a cat from under
the taxi wheels. As he landed within a foot of the curb, the front
wing grazed his arm.

"My God! That was a near squeak!"

"My own damn fault," Carne told him evenly, and was his
own quiet self again. He seemed ashamed of such an outburst
and gave another farewell nod as he stepped into the road
again. Now he looked both ways and Travers watched him to
the far curb.

But it was a puzzled Travers who walked on alone. Patrick
Carne—the placid, the steady-going, the immovable! An amazing leap that had been, and a cool brain behind it. A dark horse,
Carne. Somehow Travers had always suspected it but now he
knew. Cool as ice and quick as thought itself. In that moment of
the leap it had been as if one saw the real man, and all that convention and placidity was make-believe. And there had been a
quick question in his eyes, as if he knew he had somehow made
a slip.

Then Travers was thinking of another look he had seen a few
minutes before, that look of sneering amusement when Sonia
had mentioned lunch the following day. What on earth could
that invitation mean? True one could gather that at least the
first part of the honeymoon would be spent near town, but to
break off a honeymoon for a casual lunch, surely a most unusual
thing? But was it to be usual? She had gone out of her way to
mention—indeed she had seemed to take a sardonic delight in
mentioning—that he would not be bored. And she had got rid of
Carne in order to make that confidential whisper.

Then Travers looked up to find that he had overshot the Tube station by a good two hundred yards, and, still nodding away to himself, he slowly made his way back.

That early evening he rang up Wharton at the Yard and asked how the Stanfield Hotel affair was progressing.

"We haven't found out a thing," Wharton said. "You got anything out of that cipher?"

"It's beyond my depth," Travers told him. "Besides, if your experts are fogged, what chance do I stand?"

"We're still hunting for the code word," Wharton said. "By the way, how did the wedding go off? The papers don't seem to give much."

"Oh, much as expected."

"Was she glad of her bargain?"

Travers frowned for a moment. "You there, George? . . . you are. Well, if you ask me, she hates him like hell!"

He hung up then before he was really aware, and at once was shaking his head and feeling somewhat sheepish. Why the devil had he said such a damn silly thing over the phone? And yet it was true—in a way. Sonia's every look, word and movement told what she thought. And somehow he could hardly blame her. It was like the time when he had suggested to his nurse that she should marry the gardener. "I wouldn't have him, Master Ludo," she said, "not if he was hung all over with diamonds," And that was somehow what most women must feel about Sidley Cordovan; Sidley, with his plump sleekness, his little suspicious eyes, his complacency and his cheap way of pushing himself.

But what Travers thought that evening and what he read in the papers had little bearing on the happenings that followed. He was unusually tired that night and fell asleep almost at the moment his head met the pillow. Then practically before he was in bed at all, so it seemed, Palmer was shaking him.

"The phone, sir. You're wanted urgently!"

Travers roused himself and groped for his glasses.

"What time is it?"

"Almost six o'clock, sir."

"The devil it is," he said. "Who wants me, do you know?"

"Superintendent Wharton, sir."

Travers scurried towards the phone and as soon as he picked up the receiver, heard Wharton's little grunt.

"Yes, George; what is it?"

"Can you pick me up at the bottom of Whitehall in twenty minutes?"

"Yes . . . why?"

"Something damn serious," Wharton said. "Sonia Vorge has been murdered!"

"My God!" Travers said, and licked his lips. "Where was it?"

"That place you were telling me about on Monday. Montage Court."

He hung up then but Travers still held the receiver in his hand. Montage Court. Extraordinary how he had never thought of that.

III
THE HANGING ROPE

LUDOVIC TRAVERS, asked on a certain occasion what were his precise connections with Scotland Yard, made much the following reply.

"I'm the radio in the limousine, or a kind of unofficial gin-and-It. In other words," he said, "I keep up a flow of babble and talk about everything in sight. In fact I do so much talking that I'm bound now and again to hit on some bright idea; and if I don't, then I may stimulate or irritate the real brainy people so that they have ideas."

That piece of camouflage or leg-pulling was sufficiently near the truth to be very wide of the mark. From the very first moment of his fortunate association with Travers, George Wharton had indeed been aware that his cultured and patrician friend was fertile in ideas and prodigal of theories—and both with a difference. For Travers's ideas were always interesting in themselves, products, as they were, of a mind that was whimsically alert; while his theories were backed by so admirable a logic that truth itself seemed perverse and distorted when they unaccountably turned out to be wrong. As for the intuitions which so often startled Wharton, they were the things which should never have surprised him, sprung as they were from a keen observation, a lightning, cross-word kind of brain, an incredibly wide reading and social experience, and a lifetime's interest in one's fellow man.

But what Wharton would have described as Travers's greatest asset was the fact that he was so obviously a gentleman, and neither eccentricity nor disregard of convention could disguise the fact. His manners were so delightful and unaffected, and he was so good a listener, that he seemed to invite confidences where the officialdom and bluster of the law would altogether fail. But if Wharton had one grumble, it was this. The heart of Travers was far too tender and his pocket too much in touch with his quick sympathies. For Travers the thrill lay in deduction and unravelling; for Wharton it came at that supreme moment when he knew he had his man.

The Rolls drew in at the curb well on time that chill morning, and no sooner was Wharton in than Travers was heading her east along the embankment.

"No enormous hurry," said Wharton, always nervous of what he called Travers's hell-wagon. "Soon as the news came they routed out Norris and Lewis. They'll have been there a good hour by now."

"How was she killed?" Travers said.

"Stabbed. Died at once, I'd say."

"And what time?"

"Round about midnight, so I gathered." He grunted. "Sensible authorities down there, calling us in straightaway."

London Bridge was deserted and Travers headed south, pushing the car along, for with Wharton's well-known face at the window there was no fear of traffic police.

"Don't let me take your thoughts off the wheel," Wharton suddenly said, "but tell me one or two things, if you can."

"Carry on," Travers told him. "It's child's-play driving this time of day."

"Then about this Montage Court place. How'd the couple come to be there?"

"Were they *both* there?"

Wharton stared. "What do you mean?"

"Nothing," Travers said. "But your answer says you don't know if they were both there. The fact is I had a suspicion in my mind that there wasn't going to be a honeymoon at all."

"You don't say so!" He nodded to himself. "Sort of separation at the church door. Just an arrangement, and calling it marriage. Well"—he nodded again—"some people were right after all." Then his head swivelled round. "Just a minute, though. What was that you were telling me over the phone, about her hating him like hell?"

"That?" said Travers, and took the left turn by Lewisham clock. "That was a too hasty remark based on nothing but impressions."

Wharton grunted again. "Yes, but what impressions?"

"Well, to put it in the simplest possible thoughts just as they occur to me, I'd say she despised him and she took the fact that he knew it so much for granted that she took no pains whatever to conceal it."

"Hm!" went Wharton. "And anything else?"

"Yes," said Travers slowly. "I'm beginning at this very moment to see something else. I believe that business of his throwing her over was the only thing that ever made her lose her poise. From what I was told I believe she gave her tongue pretty free play. You see, she may be self-centred enough but that one outburst was very revealing. It showed that egomania in her. She thought the whole world was laughing behind her back. She knew she'd been made a fool of."

Wharton frowned. "I don't quite see what we're getting at."

"I'm getting at this," Travers told him. "Only three months or so ago when Cordovan threw her over, she could have murdered him. Yesterday her feelings had so far improved that she merely showed her contempt."

"Yes," said Wharton reflectively. "I think I'm beginning to see. You and I may have to do a lot of inquiring into what it was that changed her mind even that much. And, of course, why she took him back again."

Travers drew in at a direction post and turned the car left again for the open country. Wharton was busy with his thoughts, frowning prodigiously and pursing his lips. Then all at once he remembered something.

"You didn't tell me about why the honeymoon should be at this Montage Court place."

"I don't know myself," Travers said. "I can see the connections well enough, that's all. Sir Raphael was always very fond of Sonia, and Sonia was connected with Trove, and Trove, as the son of Sir Raphael's old partner, would also count. I'd say it was Sonia's idea to spend some part of the honeymoon there."

"Know what it's like?"

"I don't," Travers said. "I have an idea that part of it is what's left of an original Montage Castle, and I seem to remember that it's a rather rambling pre-Tudor place. It must be pretty large or Sir Raphael couldn't have housed his collection in it."

In a couple of minutes Wharton was telling him to stop the car, for a constable had been standing at a gate by that parkland they had just passed. Wharton was right, for the small park was the outer grounds of the house and as they came back they saw the line of chimneys beyond a tall, red-bricked wall.

"That wall's lucky," Wharton said. "Half the sensation-mongers in England'll be down here in no time."

The Rolls went through an arched gateway to a vast yard at the back of which the long rambling building lay, with its mellow roof, and twisted gables, and long latticed windows set in timbering that the centuries had bleached to grey. Three cars were there already, and no sooner was Wharton on the flagged steps than Detective-Sergeant Lewis was seen waiting in the darkness beyond the great oak door.

"How're things going?" Wharton fired.

"Not so bad, sir," Lewis said, and gave the Old General a speculative grin. "Shouldn't be surprised, sir, if we were home for dinner." He caught Travers's eye and gave a quick wink. "This way, sir. Everything's upstairs."

At that hint from Lewis that the case might soon be over, Travers's spirits had taken so sudden a sinking that he was oblivious to the beauty of that carved staircase and the intricate timbering that canopied the main hall. The zest had suddenly gone from life, so that when Norris appeared on the main landing, his nod was as grave as the Inspector's own.

"Everything ready for you, sir," Norris was saying. "We've got Mr. Cordovan in a separate room. He's more like himself now, so I should say, sir."

"It's double-Dutch to me," Wharton told him.

"Let's have a look at her first and hear what the doctor's got to say."

"Just a minute, sir," Norris said. "I'd like you to get your bearings. I think you'll find it'll save time."

At the head of those stairs lay a long and wide gallery, with what appeared to be its own timbered roof. To the left were what Norris said were the doors of bedrooms.

"There're three sets of stairs," he told Wharton. "The one you've just come up by; one from that middle door on the right— that goes down near the drawing-room and out to the walled garden; and the last at the far end there, sir, and that goes down to the servants' quarters. You'll find that middle door and staircase very important, sir."

Wharton scowled in the direction of his pointing finger, then ran his eye along the bedroom doors.

"I've got that. Now where's her room?"

"This first one, sir. We've got her out of the bed and on a table."

Wharton nodded and passed through the door that Norris held. Travers followed but kept his distance, eyes puckering with the horror of the thing his inner mind could already see. But Wharton was making straight for the table and his hand whisked back the sheet. For a long minute he stood there looking down. Menzies, the grizzled old police-surgeon, came quietly across. Wharton gave him a nod.

"Killed her at once, did it?"

"I should hardly think she moved," Menzies told him.

"Knife, or what?"

Menzies, sparing even of speech, nodded back to a side table where the knife lay. It was the black-handled kind with long triangular blade.

"Any prints on it?"

"Yes," Norris said, and his voice lowered. "Mr. Cordovan's."

"What!" Wharton stared. "You mean, her husband's!"

Norris gave a nod towards the print men as if in confirmation.

"That's right, sir. Never a shadow of a doubt."

Wharton's eyes narrowed. "And what's he say?"

"Says he doesn't know a thing."

"Oh, does he?" said Wharton grimly. "Maybe he'll soon be changing his mind. Have you anything to remark on, Menzies?"

"No," said Menzies. "I'm not prepared to say she was killed in the bed, or that she wasn't."

"I see. Got a doubt, have you?" He grunted. "And when was it done?"

"Round about midnight," Menzies told him unconcernedly.

"Photos taken?"

"All routine work done, sir," Norris said. "No prints here so far except what we can identify."

"Right," said Wharton, and made as if to replace the sheet. Menzies's voice came quickly in.

"Just a minute! I'd like you to take a squint at the wound. Round the edges here. What do you make of it?"

Travers winced while Wharton peered and fingered.

"Nice clean little job?"

"Not too clean?"

Wharton gave him a look. Menzies began some fingering on his own account.

"Just look at that now. Was it a thrust or was it just a gentle squeeze?"

Wharton shook his head. "Certainly doesn't look like a thrust. The skin's cut clean." He swivelled round. "What would it mean exactly?"

Menzies shrugged his shoulders. "Well, say she was lying in the bed there, and he came in the room—"

"Came from where?"

"Let me explain, sir," Norris cut in quickly. "Through there is a dressing-room and bathroom and lavatory, and another bedroom—the one where we've got Cordovan at this minute. It's like a suite of two bedrooms communicating through the—well, the offices in the middle."

"Good enough," Wharton said. "We'll say then he came in from the bathroom there."

"Well, if she were lying there," Menzies went on, "it would be a perfectly natural thing for him to bend over her and kiss her. The knife—if it was held properly—could then have been squeezed quickly home, not thrust home."

"You can prove it?"

"Why not?" said Menzies curtly.

"Right," said Wharton. "Better leave her here for a bit, though."

He let his eyes wander round the room, then spotted something else.

"What's that decanter and glasses doing?"

"Those came from the dressing-room," Norris said, and then gave a gentle clearing of his throat. "Look here, sir. I'd like you, if you will, to run a quick eye over everything along certain lines I've mapped out. You'll find everything fits in, sir; decanter and all."

"You should know," Wharton told him mildly. "Where do I begin?"

"A look at this room first, sir, just as it was when Coales discovered her."

"Who's Coales?"

"A retired butler, sir. He and his wife and granddaughter act as sort of caretakers here, and have done ever since Sir Raphael left England." All the time he had been moving about the room, shifting this and that and getting things to his liking. One last survey and he drew back. "There you are, sir. Say that enamelled mirror's her head on the pillow, and everything's just as it was."

Wharton took a look from two or three angles, then made only one comment.

"That reading lamp was on?" It was the double lamp, vellum shaded, attached to the head of the bed itself, at which he was pointing. "What I mean is, this room wasn't overlooked in any way, so if she was in bed and he wasn't, why shouldn't all the lights have been on?"

"That I don't know, sir. But I'll call your attention to something else. See these pillows? Well, sir, unless she tried both sides of the bed to see which she preferred, then I'd say there'd been two people in the bed."

"The devil there had!" He looked up. "What's Cordovan say about it?"

"Says he doesn't know a thing."

"Oh," said Wharton lamely. "Doesn't know a thing about that either. Anything else?"

"Yes," said Norris. "Coales found that door ajar."

It was the one by which Wharton had entered, and at once his eyes lifted to it. Then he shook his head.

"No particular reason why it should be shut. You can do what you like in your own house, and it *was* their house, for the time."

"Well, I'd like you to remember it," Norris said. "I think you're going to find it fits in with certain other peculiar things."

"Such as what?"

Norris kept a perfectly straight face. "Well, sir, for one thing—the ghost."

"Ghost!" His mouth gaped, then he grunted. "What is all this? A Lyceum pantomime?"

"You'll know very soon, sir," Norris told him imperturbably. "And now, sir, if you will, I'd like you to have a quick look at something else and then have a word with Coales."

"Pardon me a moment." Travers's voice came in for the first time. "What exactly can one see out of those windows?"

"Turn off that reading light, Doc, will you?" He swished back the curtains of the two long windows. "There you are, Mr. Travers. I think you can answer your own question."

Travers looked down on a long expanse of lawn, backed by a wall of mellow brick, along which ran what looked like herbaceous beds. A few standard trees were in early flower and daffodil clumps were sprinkled about in the grass beneath them. It was sixty yards to the far wall and behind it was a wood of beech and oak.

"That's all right," Travers said. "Nobody, of course, could have entered the room this way."

The words had held a note of inquiry. Norris and Wharton both looked down, and it was the General who gave the grunt.

"Dammit! there's a window sticking out right beneath. I wouldn't mind betting I could climb up here myself."

"There wasn't a print anywhere," Norris said. "There wasn't even a smudge."

Wharton turned to Lewis who had just come in. "Get hold of a ladder and have a look outside there. Put a man on it if you're busy."

"This way, sir," Norris said, moving to the middle door. Wharton seemed surprised at the extent of those inner rooms, with the lounge dressing-room, spacious bathroom and the twin lavatories. On a settee lay a disordered heap of women's clothes.

"She didn't bring a maid with her?" Wharton asked.

"No maid, sir. The granddaughter here was going to look after her, the short time they were staying here."

"And how long was that?"

"Till Friday, sir—so I gathered from Coales."

Wharton sneered. "Cordovan, I suppose, still knowing nothing." He moved on towards the far door. "Well, let's have a peep at him."

The door opened on a bedroom the spit of that in which Soma's body lay, except that a telephone stood on the bedside table. But the astounding thing was that on the bed, sprawled diagonally, lay Sidley Cordovan, sound asleep. One of Norris's men was seated at the bedside watching him, and up he got when Norris spoke.

"Yes, sir. He sort of lay down just as he is now, and before I knew it he was sound asleep."

"Just a minute!" Wharton bent over the sleeping man and listened. Sidley was not a handsome sight, his chubby cheeks a yellowish grey, his eyes bagged, mouth gaping, and hairy chest bulging through the wide opening of dressing gown and pyjama jacket. Wharton straightened himself and frowned.

His voice was a whisper.

"Menzies seen him yet?"

Norris shook his head.

Wharton nodded, then moved quietly to the outer door. He opened it gently and motioned the others through. The door was closed again before he spoke, and it was still in little above a whisper.

"He's either dazed or tight. He isn't sleeping normally."

"How could he be sleeping normally?" Travers asked with the same quiet. "He knows his wife is dead, Norris?"

"He knows all right, sir." Then he shook his head. "Yet I don't know if he does. He heard what I told him and blinked a bit, and sat down on that bed there and rubbed his hands through his hair, and all I could get out of him was that he didn't know."

Wharton's eyes were narrowing as he nodded to himself.

"I see. And where was he when Coales found him?"

"In that bed there, sir. Sound asleep and undressed and everything. Coales said it took him five minutes to get him awake and as soon as he left him alone again, off he went back asleep." He gave Wharton a quick look. "Coales kept trying to hint that he was dead drunk, only he didn't hardly like to say so."

"Leave that for a bit," Wharton said. "What's the next item on the menu?"

"This, sir," Norris said, and with a wave of the hand that was almost dramatic, pointed to the hanging rope.

Take three bricks and lay them along any straight edge, with an inch space between each, and then you have the precise layout of the three main suites that ran along the main gallery.

Each space was a kind of recess, and had a window with decoration of stained glass, beneath which was a carved chest. Norris drew the heavy curtains across the window of that annex where the three now stood, and switched on the light.

"This was how things were last night, sir," he said to Wharton.

But Wharton was still looking at that hanging rope. It was of the thickness of stout linen-line and hung from a cross-beam of old oak that ran from wall to wall. The beam was ten feet from the ground, and standing by the far wall was a Stuart chair. Wharton moved across at once, whipped out his glass, and had a look at the cane seat.

"Look at the edges, George," Travers said. "That cane would have burst."

"It's all right," Wharton said. "I've got it, or what ought to be it Somebody stood on this to get that rope over the beam. Was the noose tied first, or after?"

"Why was it tied at all?"

That was Travers. Wharton gave a grunt.

"Where's the mystery? Someone intended to commit suicide—isn't that plain enough? Then his nerve failed him, or he changed his mind and didn't have time to get the rope down again."

Then all at once he was turning to Norris with a look that went beyond satisfaction.

"You might even say he was too tight to hang himself! He might even have got so tight that he went off to sleep and forgot he'd made a date with that rope." He whipped round on Travers, full of the idea. "Cordovan a heavy drinker?"

Travers shrugged his shoulders.

"No more than most of his kind, I believe. I should say he could carry his liquor rather better than you're making out."

"Pardon me, sir." That was Norris. "May I suggest you see Coales. I think then, sir, you'll see things in rather a different way."

"Oh?" said Wharton belligerently. Then he grunted and his tone was all at once mild again. "Still, you ought to know. As you say, we might do worse than have a word with Coales."

IV
GHOSTS AND GLASSES

"Where's the best place to see Coales?" Wharton said.

"Up here, sir," Norris told him. "I think you'll find you'll have to bring him up here in any case." There was a man on duty at the head of the servants' stairway and he was sent for the butler. Menzies had heard voices and had come out by the far bedroom door. Wharton beckoned him across.

"I want you to wake that chap Cordovan," he said. "Get him really thoroughly awake. Make him take a cold shower, if necessary, and ring for some coffee. Then make a careful examination of him."

"What for?" asked Menzies.

Wharton smiled sardonically. "He'll be telling you what for."

The party of three moved off to the head of the far stairs, and almost at once there was the sound of approaching feet on the oak floor of the hall below.

"Any point in having the other servants up?" Wharton whispered hastily.

Norris shook his head as old Coales came into view mounting the stairs. He was a spare figure, with thin neck on which his bald head was so deeply set that at first view he had something of the appearance of a vulture. But as he came nearer one saw the face was dignified and kindly. A simple man, one might have said, but loyal, genuine and warm of heart. Wharton summed him up at once and, showman as he always was, framed the greeting accordingly.

"Mr. Coales, is it?" Out went the hand. "Very glad to see you, Mr. Coales, and to have you here to help us."

"Thank *you*, sir," the old man said, and gave a quick glance at Travers, wondering perhaps what one of his appearance should be doing. He even ventured on a question. "You're from the solicitors, sir?"

Travers smiled gravely. "I'm afraid not—that is, if you mean Sir Raphael's solicitors."

"That's all right," broke in Wharton. "And now, Mr. Coales, just a few personal questions, to enable us to see who everybody is, so to speak."

Within five minutes the position was perfectly clear. Coales and his wife had been in the service of the Breyes all their lives. Five years before, when Sir Raphael took up that final residence in France, Coales had reached his seventieth year and was thereupon pensioned off and given the sinecure post of caretaker at Montage Court, with his granddaughter to help with the work. That, in fact, was little, for only one suite of bedrooms was kept up, and downstairs most of the furniture and every picture of value had been removed. There were only two gardeners where there had once been five, and they were also pensioners. All the staff was paid by the solicitors—Marribun and Clite—with Coales as a kind of sub-agent.

"About last night," Wharton said, and his face took on a due gravity. "Tell us what happened from the time Mr. and Mrs. Cordovan got here."

"Well, sir, the bags were taken up and my granddaughter helped Mrs. Cordovan to do some unpacking and then I served tea myself in the drawing-room. Then Mr. Cordovan walked in the grounds for a time, sir, and Mrs. Cordovan read a book and some magazines—illustrated magazines, sir."

"Yes," said Wharton. "Carry on."

"They didn't actually change for dinner, sir, and I brought in sherry at a quarter past seven and dinner was at half-past." He thought then for a moment. "Coffee and kümmel, sir, and it was at about nine when they went to the billiard-room. Mr. Cordovan told me not to wait up, sir, but he asked me to place a decanter and siphon upstairs—which I did, sir."

"Yes?"

"And then, sir, Mrs. Cordovan came back from the billiard-room and began talking to me confidentially. She said she was very worried about him, sir, because he walked a good deal in his sleep. It was usually about midnight when it happened, sir, and she said would I be sure to take a quick look in the bedroom at about that time and make sure he was still there. She was leaving the door ajar for that purpose, sir."

"A most unusual request, surely?"

Coales bowed. "Well, sir, I'm telling you precisely what occurred. I did look in at the billiard-room just before ten but Mr. Cordovan said there was nothing they wanted, and Mrs. Cordovan said they were just going up. I'd already locked up everywhere, sir, so we retired to bed. I may say, sir, that I set an alarm clock by my bedside for ten minutes to twelve."

"You and your wife occupied the same room?"

"Yes, sir, and my granddaughter was in the room just beyond. The east wing, it is, sir."

His manner was getting slightly agitated and Wharton steadied him.

"Take it easy, Mr. Coales. No hurry. Simply tell us what happened when the alarm went off—that is, if it didn't happen before."

Coales shook his head. "It was after it went off, sir. I put on a dressing gown, sir, and came up these stairs. I'd switched on the light from the bottom, sir, but it wasn't very strong." He licked his lips. "I'd just got to here, sir, where I'm standing now, when I saw it."

"Saw what?"

"The ghost, sir." He caught the faint look on Wharton's face and drew himself up with a quaint dignity. "The Lame Monk of Montage, sir."

Wharton pursed his lips. "The Lame Monk of Montage. Quite a well-known ghost, then." He raised an admonitory finger. "Don't mistake me, Mr. Coales. I'm believing you implicitly. But you did speak as if the ghost were well-known; isn't that so?"

"The ghost is well-known, sir. It has been seen on many occasions and it always means death."

"Just a moment," said Travers. "I'm beginning to recall something. Tell me, Coales; did Mr. Philip Carne ever have anything to do with the ghost?"

The old man's face beamed. "You're right, sir—he did. He put the ghost in a play, sir, and he came down here on purpose to talk to me about him, sir. Afterwards he presented me with a copy, sir, signed by himself. I can fetch it, sir, if you wish."

"I think I remember it," Travers told him. "It was called *The Stooping Churl*, or some such title." He smiled over at the old butler. "Wasn't it about a monk who'd been thrown from a monastery wall and lamed, and didn't he take service at the castle disguised as a jester?"

Coales rubbed gratified hands. "That was it, sir. And he killed the baron, sir."

"Well, you tell us just what you saw," Wharton said. "Stand just where you did last night, and everything."

Coales took up a position at the head of the stairs. "Here's where I was, sir, and I saw him so suddenly, sir, I hadn't time to think. My blood froze and I tried to shriek, sir, but I couldn't."

"Where was he when you saw him? Let Mr. Travers here go to where he was. You direct him."

Travers went back along the gallery, directed by the old man's voice, and at last was halted just on the far side of the central stairway.

"Now describe him," Wharton said.

"He was dark, sir. I could hardly see him at all, except his face and that was all lit up and shining, sir. Unearthly, you might call it. It was a pale face, sir, with the jaw sticking out, and just as I stood there, sir, he moved towards the stairs and disappeared. There wasn't a sound, sir. And he gave a limp, sir, as he moved, and soon as he had gone, sir, I got my strength back again and bolted down the stairs and into my bedroom, sir. Even then I couldn't speak for a minute, sir, and then I told my wife. 'It's death,' she said, and she was as frightened as I was, sir. 'It's death,' she said. 'The gentleman has been walking in his sleep and fallen out of a window and killed himself.'"

"I see." Wharton thought for a good long minute, then nodded. "Well, now tell us what happened then."

"Well, sir, I remembered my duty and I came back again, and as soon as I got here, sir, I switched on this light so that I could see right along the gallery. Then I gave a little tap at the bedroom door, sir, and peeped in, and you could have knocked me down with a feather, sir, when I saw madame all alone, and I thought my wife was right. I stayed for a minute, sir, then I went in." He shook his head. "I was going to wake her, sir, and tell her. Then I saw . . . well, sir, I saw her lying there."

He was overcome for a moment. Wharton nodded sympathetically.

"And then you went through to the phone and saw Mr. Cordovan asleep. That must have been a shock to you too."

"It was, sir. And then I couldn't waken him, sir." Wharton nodded some more, then his hand fell on the old man's shoulder.

"You're what we call a good witness, Mr. Coales. Now we'll forget everything—except the ghost. Let's go along to Mr. Travers."

Modern doors, closely swung and disguised as old oak, were at the head of that central stairway. Wharton tried them and found them noiseless, but however carefully he moved his feet, there was a sound on the oak flooring, audible to Norris even at the corridor end from which they had just come.

"Show us the way downstairs," Wharton said to Coales. "Don't think me sceptical but I'd prefer to think the ghost didn't float on air."

The stairway went down to a landing, turned left and in one more flight came out at the drawing-room, a fine, large room that looked out on the gardens. Coales halted for instructions. Wharton made for the main door and tried it.

"This just as you left it last night?"

Coales took a look and said that it was. Wharton ran his eyes over the windows.

"A ghost couldn't have got through them, open or shut," he said. "But what's that door there?"

It was the door to a small inner room, once used, so Coales said, as a private den by Sir Raphael. Wharton took a look inside, then moved over to another door that also appeared to lead to the gardens. It had a hanging metal handle, and as he turned it and pulled, the door opened, and there beneath his eyes was the flagged path. He stared blankly for a moment, then whipped round on Coales. Coales was staring too.

"I closed it, sir. I'll swear it was closed."

"That's all right," Wharton told him genially. "Nothing to worry about." He waved him back. "I don't want you treading about round here. In fact, I think we can spare you altogether for a little while. Perhaps you'll give us the official statement later." He turned to Travers and Norris. "Any questions?"

Norris shook his head, then thought of one.

"I suppose Mr. Coales couldn't tell us what size the ghost was? What height, if he likes."

Coales shook his head. "I couldn't tell you, sir. It was just a figure, sir. Just like something in the dark. And the face, all lighted—it confused me, sir."

Norris nodded. Travers cut in.

"Mr. Patrick Carne and his mother came here frequently?"

Coales smiled. "Why, yes, sir. When Sir Raphael was in evidence. Neither has been much since, sir. Mrs. Carne called about a month ago—a friendly visit to myself and my wife, if I may say so, sir."

"Of course. Mr. Cordovan knew it very well too?"

"Certainly, sir. If I may say so, all the family were very often here."

"Including the lady I now call Miss Sonia Vorge?" The old man shook a reflective head. "Sir Raphael was very attached to Miss Vorge, sir."

"So I believe," Travers told him. "But one last question. All the family knew about the ghost?"

"The ghost, sir, is *part* of the family," Coales said, and with a tremendous dignity.

Wharton watched the door close on him, then pursed out lips of contempt.

"Ghost! Lame Monk of Montage! Lame Monk—my eye! How many men have you got, Norris? Enough to hunt inside and out? If so, get it going straightaway. Meet us upstairs outside the door by that rope."

He moved off that way with Travers at his heels, and he was still muttering about damned old fools, and humbug.

"I don't think you ought to be bigoted," Travers told him gently. 'Finer people than myself and you, George, have seen ghosts. Incredulity never was argument."

Wharton stopped there on the landing and glared.

"Now you're talking humbug. Can you look me in the face and say you know that old fool saw a ghost?"

Travers shook his head. "Now you're being reasonable. What I'll say is that if on any other occasion Coales had sworn he'd seen the Montage ghost, I'd have believed him—with possible reservations. But last night—well, no."

"That's all right then," Wharton said mildly. His tone took on a faint suspicion. "Who were those Carnes you were asking him about?"

Travers found an old envelope and drew a rough family tree, and by the time Norris was with them again, Wharton said he had the Breyes at his fingers' ends. Then he listened for a moment outside Cordovan's door, gave a quick look of surprise and then walked in. The room was empty but Menzies' voice could be heard in the inner lounge. Wharton listened again before turning the handle.

Sidley Cordovan was sitting on the low chesterfield, head cupped in his hands, and he looked up almost idly as the three entered. Menzies rose quickly from the chair.

"This is Superintendent Wharton, Mr. Cordovan."

But it was at Travers that Cordovan was staring.

"What're you doing here, Travers?"

"Just come to see if I could help," Travers told him, and smiled. "How're you feeling now? More like yourself?"

Cordovan shook his head and once more his fingers began a frantic running through his whitish yellow hair.

"I can't think. . . . Dammit! if only I could think!"

Wharton stood looking down at him, and suddenly his lip curled.

"You're a fine actor, Mr. Cordovan."

"What's that?" He looked up.

"I say you're a fine actor."

He moistened his lips, then his jaws clamped together and Travers thought he was going to spring. Then Wharton was all at once laughing quietly.

"Just my little joke. Trying to get you to take a hold of yourself." His hand fell on the other's shoulder. "It's a terrible thing—we all know that. Still, we've all got our duty."

Once more Cordovan's head was in his cupped hands, and he was shaking his head and blinking, as if trying in some queer way to think. As Travers saw, he still looked desperately ill, though the unshaven chin and the dressing gown gave a slovenliness that set as in relief the baggy eyes and the sallow of the cheeks.

"Mr. Cordovan is much better than he was," Menzies said. "He's been drugged, but he's got some of it out of his system."

"Drugged!" said Wharton, and over Cordovan's head gave a quick look that was something of the nature of an elaborate wink. "That's pretty bad. And who did the drugging?"

"Tell the Superintendent about it," Menzies said, like a father.

"Yes," said Wharton, and drew himself up a chair. "Take your own time about it, but tell us what happened after you got up here last night. What room did you come into, for instance?"

"I remember that all right," he said. "We—"

The one word was enough, and his head went down again.

"I can't tell you. . . . I can't do it."

"Oh, my God!" wailed Wharton. His hands spread. "Mr. Cordovan, do you think we don't all sympathize with you? I know just what you're going through, but still—" He clicked his tongue, then his hands were waving again. "Don't you want us to get the man who killed her? That's what we're here for, and how can we do it if you don't help us?"

A moment or two and Cordovan was lifting his head.

"All right," he said wearily. "What do you want me to say?"

"That's better," Wharton said. "Just begin at when you came up last night."

"Well"—he was to speak very slowly, and jerkily—"we came in here, through that room there. We sat for a bit, and talked, and then she poured herself a drink." His eyes opened, almost craftily. "That's it. She was pouring a drink and I said, 'You might as well give me one too.'"

"Let me see," said Wharton reminiscently. "It was you who told Coales to bring drinks up here, wasn't it?"

"What's that?" He shook his head. "She told me and I told Coales."

Wharton nodded. "And what happened then; I mean, after you'd had the drink?"

"I don't know. I tell you I don't know." His eyes were puckering and his head was shaking as if with fright. Menzies made a quick sign to Wharton.

"That's all right, Mr. Cordovan," Menzies said. "Don't do any more thinking. Don't worry about anything. It'll all come back in time."

"Just one little question," Wharton said, and got to his feet. "When did you first begin to suffer from sleep-walking, Mr. Cordovan?"

He looked quickly up at that. "Sleep-walking?"

Wharton smiled sympathetically. "Yes, sleepwalking. You do walk in your sleep at times, don't you?"

He shook his head. "Not that I know of." The eyes opened frightenedly. "Who told you that?"

Wharton gave a little laugh. "There, that's better. Only another of my little jokes."

His hands went down and he was helping the unresisting Cordovan to his feet.

"That's right. Feel better? Of course you do. And now let me prescribe for you. You and the Doctor go down and have breakfast together. Oh, I know! I know you don't feel like eating a thing. Every bite's going to choke you. . . . Come along, Doc! Take him downstairs and get over the fire and try some coffee and toast. . . . That's it. That's it."

The outer door closed on the two, and at once his face dramatically changed.

"Quick, Norris! Get what help you can and go through these rooms with a small-tooth comb. If there was a drug, it was kept in something. Pick up anything else you can. Mr. Travers and

I will have a look out on the lawns there, to see if the bottle or anything was thrown."

"Just one minute first, sir," Norris said. "He just told you she poured herself a drink and then he had one himself, and after that he knew nothing."

"Well?" said Wharton belligerently.

"Well, it's wrong, sir. Only one of those two glasses had been drunk out of!"

"You're sure?"

"Dead sure, sir."

"What about the prints?"

"Hers on the glass that had been drunk out of, sir."

"What about the other?"

Norris smiled confidently. "None at all, sir."

"And you're sure of that?"

"Yes, sir. Never a print."

"Right," said Wharton, moving towards the door. "Get some men quick and go over these rooms." Then at the very door he halted to throw his bombshell. "While you're doing it, ask yourself this. If there weren't any prints, what happened to the ones Coales left on when he put that glass on the tray?"

V
TRAVERS REMEMBERS

THEY HAD GONE out through Cordovan's room, but no sooner were they in the annex than Wharton was opening the door again.

"I'd rather like to have a look at that glass myself," he said.

Travers followed him through the lounge dressing-room to the first bedroom. The sun was now out and coming through the lozenge panes of the old windows, so that but for the table and the outline of that something that lay beneath the sheet, the room would have been gay and colourful. Wharton put on his gloves and made for the tray.

"Never a print there," he said, holding the one glass to the light. "Hasn't been drunk out of either." He lifted the other, sniffed at it, then held it up. "This one's all right. Can't say how much it held, though." Then he looked up. "I suppose Cordovan couldn't have been the only one to have a drink? If so, there'd be some of the drug in this moisture at the bottom. Think I'll mention it to Menzies."

Norris's bag was still in the room and he helped himself to a quarto envelope.

"Let's have a look in the bathroom," he said to Travers. "I've got an idea."

Travers knew well enough what the idea was. Two glasses might have been used, and then one carefully washed and polished, and if so the bathroom would have been the place for the cleaning. But the trouble turned out to be the multitude of towels, for all sorts were there, used and unused: small towels of linen, face towels, bath towels, and a tiny hanging towel for razors. Wharton clicked his tongue annoyedly.

"What people want to be always bathing and washing themselves for, beats me. Too much time on their hands, that's what it is. Nothing in there, I suppose?"

But that corner linen-basket did hold something—three wet towels and among them a soiled linen one. Wharton grabbed that latter at once, held it up, then looked at Travers.

"That's the one for a fiver," Travers said. "It's been screwed up just as you do screw up a towel when you clean a glass."

Wharton folded it and put it in the envelope, then wrote something on the back. As they came out Norris was going through to Cordovan's room with two of his men.

"Plenty of men now, sir," he said. "Lewis can't find a thing outside those windows, by the way."

"All the better," Wharton told him. "The best-class ghosts don't use windows. Get this sent off to the Yard for me while I do some phoning. Mr. Travers, I'll meet you outside that drawing-room door in about five minutes."

Travers made his way downstairs and watched for a minute or two while Lewis and a couple of men went methodically over oak floors and Persian strips for footmarks. Wharton came down sooner than expected, and Lewis approached him at once.

"Something I'd like you to see, sir. Just outside the door here."

"No prints?" Wharton said. "None on the doors or anywhere?"

"Not one, sir. And the funny thing is that Coales's aren't on the door either, and yet he said he locked the place up!"

Wharton seemed more pleased than otherwise, and he was nodding away to himself as he came to that outer door of the den. What Lewis had to show were two tiny collections of what looked like gravel. Wharton was on his knees at once and poring over them with his glass.

"What do you think they are?" he asked Lewis.

Lewis's answer was involved and deductive.

"Well, if they're gravel, sir, they came off the front drive before you get to the stone-paved yard. And if so, sir, then they're off someone's boots. Then there's the way they lie, sir, as if the boots were heels to the door. And no one would stand like that, sir, with his feet close together, so it must have been a pair of boots or shoes standing here."

"Well, well, well!" said Wharton, and grimaced delightedly. "What do you think, Mr. Travers?"

"I can't see a flaw," Travers said. "It's lucky this corner's sheltered and there was no wind."

"Get them photographed and take rough measurements," Wharton told Lewis. "Then work your way round to the drive and keep your eyes out for any more."

He gave a nod to Travers and they stepped out to the flagged path and left to the drawing-room door. There he halted and cocked an ear.

"About this drug business," he said to Travers. "Any hopes of finding the container?"

Travers shook his head. "My own idea is that if we'd been meant to find it, then we'd have found it."

Wharton grunted. "You're a bit ahead of me there. What I've been thinking is that if he drugged himself, then he'd have got rid of the container. A tiny thing probably and he could have put it down the lavatory. If she did the drugging, and then was murdered before she had time to conceal it, then we might find it."

"And what about the ghost?"

"Yes," said Wharton reflectively; "there's the ghost. A hell of a business, don't you think so? First something's plain as daylight; then it's clear as mud."

A peering head appeared round the drawing-room door. It was Menzies and when he spotted them he came over.

"He won't eat anything," he said. "He's had some more coffee, though."

Wharton told him about the dregs in the glass. Menzies smiled.

"You're too late. I collected about ten drops myself. And I gave him an emetic and collected something else."

"Any idea what it was?"

"Wouldn't like to say," Menzies told him. "Whatever it was it knocked him down like the kick of a mule. You mayn't believe it but his pupils are still dilated. Now what about getting her away? The ambulance has been here an hour and more."

"Why not?" Wharton said. "One or two things I'm rather anxious to find out. Whether she was drugged, for one thing."

Menzies shook his head. "I couldn't find traces." He sighed. "Still, you never know. If nothing goes wrong I'll ring up in an hour or so—*virgo intacta* and everything." He moved off, then turned back. "You needn't worry about him. He's tucked up on a settee before the fire with a sedative inside him."

"Callous old devil!" Wharton said, as the Doctor disappeared. Then he heaved a pious sigh. "Still, there's all sorts of jobs it wouldn't do to blush over. Wonder where Coales is. There's something I'd like to know."

They went through the now open door of the drawing-room and Coales appeared at the push of the bell.

"Just one little thing," Wharton said. "Who informed you that the honeymoon was going to be spent here?"

"Mr. Marribun, sir; Mr. Edgar Marribun."

"I see. And who told him?"

"He told me, sir, that he'd had instructions from Sir Raphael direct."

Wharton grunted. "And the couple themselves. Did they say anything about it last night?"

Coales smiled. "Before that, sir. Miss Sonia—as she was then, sir—came here personally a week ago to look round again, sir, and see that everything was as she wanted it." He coughed gently. "I had instructions from her, sir, not to mention the visit to a soul."

Wharton nodded. "And what was said last night?"

"Well, sir, Mr. Cordovan said they were going to Egypt after their short stay here. He said they both needed a rest, sir, before what he called, sir, a strenuous time. In Egypt, he meant, sir, so I gathered."

"That's all then," Wharton said, and then as he turned, "I suppose, by the way, that neither your wife nor granddaughter heard anything suspicious in the night?"

"Neither did, sir."

"Good. And in all seriousness, was last night the first time you ever saw the Montage ghost?"

"The first time, sir," Coales said, and gave a little bow. "Sir Raphael saw it once, sir, many years ago; and Mrs. Cordovan, sir—Mr. Sidley's late mother. If I may venture to say so, sir, the last occasion I mentioned is in a book. It's called *Authentic Ghosts of England*, sir. We had a copy here, sir, but it was lost."

"Thank you, Mr. Coales; thank you," Wharton said, and watched till the door closed on him. "We might get Norris for a quick conference and then ask the old boy to put the kettle on. Is that clock right?"

"It says half-past eight," Travers told him, "but my innards make it later."

"Another ten minutes and we'll be having a scratch meal," Wharton said, and led the way upstairs.

Norris had found nothing during that search of the honeymoon suite. Wharton suggested that three of his men should search the vicinity of the entrance to the Court for traces of a car that had been drawn up, and any houses by the roadside might be questioned for the sound of a car at soon after midnight.

"Not that that'll help a lot," he said. "It's the number of the car that we want, or prints of the tyres."

By the time Norris was ready, Wharton had got in touch with the local police for additional help, but it was nine o'clock before the brief conference began.

"There's no point in beating about the bush," Wharton said. "I'll lay all my cards on the table and if you both do the same, then we'll compare notes."

Wharton and Norris might have been termed the analytic and the synthetic. Norris's way was to build up a case by patient, exhaustive inquiry, hoarding facts like a jackdaw. Wharton's was the method of elimination; a series of exhaustive tests of suspects followed by a gradual discarding. As for Travers, he had no method at all, save what might have been called a continuous one, which meant that he browsed here and there and waited for the unusual before focusing his mind.

"One thing we can't get away from," Wharton said, "and that's the knife. The prints seemed to me to be pretty good."

"A bit smudgy, sir, but good enough," Norris said.

"Well, you expect that sort of print to be smudgy," Wharton told him. "The fingers don't come away clean. Still, there we are. How's he going to explain away the knife? When he gets his senses back, will he claim someone put his prints on the knife while he was lying there drugged?"

"Looks as if we'll have to get his medical history," Norris said.

"The family history's none too good, according to Mr. Travers. They say old Sir Raphael's clear off his nob, and there was Evelyn Breye, this one's mother. They hushed it up but she went potty, as everyone knew."

"I think that was rather a case of bad nervous collapse," Travers said. "I admit the family's a queer one."

"Well, did he have a brainstorm, or didn't he?" fired Wharton. "If he did, then he did some pretty sensible things afterwards, such as putting up that rope, taking the drug to give him dutch courage, and so on. It may have been he who had to pretend to be the ghost when Coales suddenly popped up. If he had brain enough for all that, why was he such a fool as to leave his prints on the knife?"

"As far as I'm concerned," Travers said, "I refuse to admit that Sidley Cordovan has that kind of brain at all. He's shrewd in controlling his concerns and affairs and the very devil at a bargain. Self first and self last—that's Sidley. For instance, I'm prepared to wager that if you hint to him that it was his wife who drugged him—say in order to evade the bonds of full matrimony—then you'll see the real Sidley."

"But *did* she drug the drink?"

"We've no evidence. If you believe what he says, then she must have drugged him. There's motive for it."

"Very well," said Wharton. "You give us your version."

"For what it's worth, it's this. All along she never intended the marriage should be consummated. I speak very frankly but it's no use mincing words. I'd say she intended to make it appear that on the night of their wedding he made himself so drunk that he had to spend the night in his own room. Why did she make up that tale about sleep-walking? So that Coales should look in the room and see her alone. Then she'd have said, 'Oh, no. Mr. Cordovan isn't sleep-walking. He's beastly drunk. Look in there and you'll see him. I had to undress him myself and get him to bed.' Maybe the drugging was a bit too strong, because, as we know, he isn't himself even yet; but normally he should have recovered sufficiently this morning to have waked up in time to see her preparing to leave forever. Can't you imagine the indignant scene? And Coales as a witness?" He hesitated the merest moment. "And now I'll tell you something you don't know. Yesterday afternoon she whispered to me immediately after the ceremony that I was to lunch with her at her flat, and she promised I should be amused. Why should she be at her flat instead of here, on her honeymoon? Because she'd planned it all out. I was to be amused—ironically, of course—by the tale of Sidley's wedding night."

Wharton had been staring. Now he gave an emphatic nod.

"You're right. What do you say, Norris?"

"Fits like a glove," Norris said.

"Well, I've only one comment to make," went on Travers. "I told you yesterday in so many words that I didn't think there'd be any honeymoon. If she was under any sort of compulsion to marry him—he, of course, understanding marriage in the completest sense—then she fulfilled the contract as far as going through the actual ceremony. Then she led him on right up to the time when they entered this very room. Then she did what she'd planned, which was to make him the laughing-stock of London, just as she imagined he'd made her when he jilted her over the Trove affair."

"She must have been a regular hell-cat," Norris said.

"Feline—yes," Travers said. "I believe that when she made up her mind to a thing, nothing would have stopped her."

"Where's this flat of hers?" asked Wharton.

"At Hendon," Travers said. "It was merely a *pied-à-terre*. When she wasn't actually flying she was here and everywhere."

"Any servants?"

"It's a service flat," Travers said. "She has a personal maid there."

"Right," said Wharton. "She and I'll be having a few words together in the course of the next hour. Now let's get on to when he was drugged and she undressed him and got him on the bed. A pretty tough job, by the way, for one of her size and a heavy man like him. Still, we'll leave that. Then what? If we build round your theory, Mr. Travers, then we discard all faking of his, such as pretending to be the ghost."

"What we've got to do," said Norris, "is to try and work out what happened when he was on the bed and she got back to her own room." He thought of something. "Say, between a quarter past eleven and midnight."

"The first thing she did was clean that glass," Wharton said. "The next morning she could have pointed out to Coales that only one glass had been drunk out of, and that was her husband's. I don't know what she did next. The drug might have been in tablet form and she might have had the tablets in her bag, and if so there wouldn't be any question of getting rid of a bottle. There was nothing in her bag, was there?"

"Only the usual," Norris said. "My idea is that she lay in bed waiting for Coales, and went clean off to sleep."

"Which brings us to the ghost," went on Wharton. "We know how he got *out*, by the way, but how did he get in?"

"It was a Yale lock and he might have had a duplicate key."

"Yes," said Wharton, "there's something in that. After all, he took off his shoes and left them against the door so we ought to assume he entered by the door. He had a small torch and he made his way up here. Then what happened?"

"It's all surmise," Travers said. "But he must have come in through Cordovan's room—thinking it was unoccupied perhaps—and seen him lying there incapable. Then he went through to her room, saw her asleep and stabbed her, faking the prints either before or after—" He broke off. "No, it couldn't have been after. That would have meant withdrawing the knife or carting Cordovan to the bedside."

"The rest is easy," Wharton told them. "He left by the door of her room and just as he was nearing the staircase he saw the first corridor light was on, and he heard Coales coming up the stairs. I'd say he froze stiff against the wall, then thought of a wild chance. So he flashed his torch in his own face, thrust out his lower jaw, or put his free hand over it, gave a limp or two and nipped through the doors and down the stairs in his stockinged feet."

Norris had been nodding to himself. Now he gave a final nod of gratification.

"We know where to look then, gentlemen. It must have been a member of the family, or he wouldn't have known about the ghost."

He had given Travers a look of inquiry, and Wharton's eyes were lifting inquiringly too.

"The full list would be this," Travers said. "The two Carnes—Philip and Patrick—and their mother;

Sir Raphael himself, and Cordovan, whom we've agreed to rule out."

Wharton shook his head. "The mother can be ruled out too, and Sir Raphael's in France—or he ought to be. That leaves only the two Carnes, and it's too easy." He shrugged his shoulders. "Still, there we are. We might do worse than begin on the two Carnes. Which is your favorite, Mr. Travers?"

"Just a moment," Travers said. "I've got the idea we're rushing too far ahead. Let's look at something else before we commit ourselves. X—the murderer—couldn't possibly have known he was going to find the married couple in different rooms. It must have been a tremendous surprise when he turned the handle and walked into what he thought was an empty room, and then found Cordovan there. We know he'd come to kill someone because he'd brought the knife, but whom had he come to kill? Him, or her, or both? I must put the point because when you ask me which of the two Carnes I fancy, I have to weigh that question against motive. Are we looking for an enemy of his, or hers, or of both?"

"It'd be hard to answer that," Norris said.

"I know," Travers told him. "If we could answer all the questions, there'd hardly be a case to solve. But you know, George, that it was him I expected to be killed. Mind you, I didn't expect *anybody* to be killed, but what I'm getting at is that she hated him and he idolized her. She had a revenge to get and he hadn't. I don't see why she should have had enemies, whereas he's the kind who makes them as he goes along."

"How's that bear on the case?"

"Well, the chances are that X came to kill him. Then he saw a better way out by killing her and trying to make Cordovan out to be the murderer. He added the suicide touch by tying up that rope, and, of course, he pressed Cordovan's prints on the knife."

"Just a minute," said Wharton. "That implies that he brought the rope with him!"

Travers shook his head reprovingly. "My dear George, you can't expect perfection. We've had no time for real thinking. The rope may have come in the luggage or round it, and X may have seen it and so got the idea. He may have picked it up outside; in fact, anything may have happened."

Wharton grunted, then looked up. "Well, can you answer the question now? Who's your first suspect?"

"The two Carnes undoubtedly," Travers said. "Whoever had that sudden brainwave of incriminating Cordovan in the murder of his wife, had wits that worked quicker than lightning, and a brain as cool as ice. For all he knew, Cordovan was only dead drunk, and even dead drunks may come suddenly round. What I mean there is that he didn't know *how long* Cordovan had been drunk." He paused for a moment's thought. "In view of one other factor, I'd say my favorite was Patrick Carne."

"What factor?"

"He was a witness at the wedding, therefore he was the one who was likely to know the honeymoon was being spent here. That's the most vital factor of all."

"Yes," said Wharton, and frowned in thought. Then he looked up again.

"Well, we'd better get moving. Will you try the two Carnes, Mr. Travers, and test alibis?"

"I'll have a shot at it," Travers told him. "It's going to be a somewhat awkward business."

"Rubbish!" He gave a look at Norris. "We know better, don't we, Norris? Once Mr. Travers undertakes a job, then it's done, and done damn well."

Travers smiled. "Thanks for the lubrication, George, but this time I happen to know. When shall I start, by the way?"

"Why, now," Wharton said. "I'll get up to that Hendon flat and pick up what I can there. Everything down here is Norris's funeral; you and I'll do what we can from outside." He thought for a moment. "Anything you have to communicate, send it here to Norris." He was on the move at once. "See you later then."

Travers shook a doleful head. "I doubt if I'll be back much before evening." He halted at the door. "Do you know, I rather want to be here tonight. We've never caught the atmosphere of this place as it was last night, round about midnight I think our brains'll work much better if we can reproduce last night's conditions."

"Of course, of course," Wharton told him placatingly. "Get yourself some breakfast, by the way. Don't forget that."

A nod and a smile and Travers had gone. Then before Wharton had time to open his mouth, the door was opening again.

"George, I've just thought of something."

"Oh?" said Wharton. "And what's that?"

"The people who knew about the Montage ghost. Those who might have had a grievance against either him or her—particularly her. We've left one out!"

"Oh? And who's that?"

"Maurice Trove."

Wharton stared, then his hands went dramatically to heaven.

"Isn't that enough to infuriate you? How the hell'd I come to forget all about that!"

VI
TRAVERS INQUIRES

COALES WAS IN the main hall when Travers came down, and on the spur of the moment Travers asked him a question.

"That decanter upstairs, Coales. How full was it last night when you left it there?"

"Quite full, sir," Coales said. "I opened a special bottle for the occasion."

A happy confirmation, thought Travers. The decanter now contained about a quarter, so that the best part of three-quarters of a bottle had been poured away, and that much, according to Sonia's evidence, her husband would have drunk. The siphon, if he remembered rightly, was about half full, which would have meant that Sidley had been taking his whiskey almost neat.

And yet somehow he felt that ingenious as Sonia's scheme had been, there was a something lacking. That revenge which she had apparently planned seemed comparatively innocuous, depending for its publicity, as it did, on what would be given in court as reasons for an application for a separation, unless, of course, she had proposed to call in the press and tell them the tale. But even then the plan hardly seemed the full Sonia. It lacked the deadly feline quality and the cold vindictiveness, and the chief thing wherein it was lacking was in its success, for it was scarcely like Sonia to plan and fail.

But with the day's encounters before him, Travers put Montage Court from his mind. What he was now proposing was to call at Severns, with the hope of finding Philip Carne and with the practical certainty of seeing Henrietta. But since his best way lay through Sevenoaks he was also proposing to get some sort of a meal there. Sevenoaks was six miles from Montage, and three miles beyond Sevenoaks was Brimbald village on the outskirts of which was Severns, Henrietta's home since her husband's death.

Travers let the car crawl towards the center of the town and kept his eyes about him for a tea-shop, and it was as he caught sight of one and drew the Rolls in to the curb, that he spotted Henrietta Carne. She had been driving an ancient baby car, of the type once so dear to the comic artists, and when he first saw her she was closing its door. Then she steadied herself for a moment with her stick, and with a couple of books under her arm, moved off at a good enough pace towards the lending library.

There was a bay window in the tea-shop and he took a seat there, and as he waited for his coffee, kept an eye out for the reappearance of Henrietta. At the back of his mind was some mild amusement for the frights she had once been capable of giving him, and there was also a certain pleasure that her rheumatism was so much better that she could drive her tiny car again and walk at quite a stirring pace.

His coffee came, with cold ham and bread and butter, and then Henrietta reappeared, making straight back to the car. He watched the methodical way in which she first held herself upright by the door, then put in the stick and the books, and then with a sideways slithering ingratiated herself into the seat. Maybe she had more shopping to do, and maybe not. In any case it would be as well to linger out the meal and give her ample time to get back to Severns.

Age mellows most things, so that the domineering tyrants of our youth may seem to our minds no more than the queer and the quaint, and come in time to be recalled with a vague and tolerant affection. But Travers could feel little of affection for Henrietta Carne, and in any case affection was a thing she would have despised.

But there was an enormous deal to admire in her, and it must have been an immense fortitude that could emerge with cynicism and assurance from the upheaval that followed her husband's sudden death. Money had poured in while he was alive, but it had also poured out. That house in Marlborough Square had been a kind of society rendezvous, and few notabilities, or even notorieties, but had entered its doors. In those days there had been footmen in blue and silver liveries, with a carriage or two or a car always waiting, and sooner or later dapper Wilfred himself at the door, ushering out a sitter with gallantry and personal flourish. But it was Henrietta—and Raphael—who had made him; everybody knew that. Some said it was she who had engineered that highly profitable quarrel with the Academy, and but for his untimely death, it would certainly have been she who would have engineered his knighthood.

And now, what? Henrietta, with two maids—or was it three?—ruling that rustic roost of a house which looked as if it had begun life as a vicarage and had since covered its shame with Virginia creeper. But still indomitable—no doubt about that. Once, when Wilde was still the fashion, some supposed wit had christened her Augustus, but there was little of the male about her. *Henrietta* suited her admirably, for Henriettas seemed thinnish, hard and self-assured. Perfect assurance, that was Henrietta Carne; sure that the old had always been the best, and that experience was life's all-embracing asset. The past was her vindication and her monument. She would give a sneer perhaps, but never a lament, for her mellowing had been into a cynical acceptance of the new; with a silent toleration of that new because it so patently lacked each virtue and achievement of the old.

It was nearer eleven than ten when Travers went out to the car again, and once more he took his time. Severns, he remem-

bered, lay on the Sevenoaks side of the village, and off the se-
cluded by-road in country comparatively flat. As he had a new
glimpse of it from the gate of the short drive, it seemed to have
suffered no change. There was the same creeper hiding the stuc-
co, and there were the lawns with their formal beds that in summer would be hectic with geraniums and blue lobelia. Yet there
had been a change. That odd room at the end of the rambling
house had been made into a garage for Henrietta's car, for the
doors were open and there was the car itself. A good idea that,
and only a yard or two for Henrietta to walk from the porch with
her game leg.

The front door was open and as he came to it, Henrietta appeared in the tiny hall. Her eyes opened at the sight of him.

"Well!—Ludovic Travers!"

"How do you do, Mrs. Carne," he said. "May I come in?"

"My dear boy!" There was reproach in the tone, and she was
opening at once a door on the left. Travers entered what he remembered to be the drawing-room, with its serried pictures by
the late Wilfred, and above the marble mantelpiece the huge
portrait of Henrietta as a debutante.

"Put your things down here," she said, and took a seat by
the fire. "Sit down and talk to me. Tell me why you've made this
sudden appearance."

"Tell me about yourself," he said. "How are you? Very much
better?"

"Quite better," she told him decisively. "I've had that new
heat treatment and the rheumatism is now confined to this one
knee. You're looking very well, Ludovic."

"Perhaps I am," he said. "All I can hope is that age will deal
as well with me as it has with you."

"You're your father again," she told him, not ungratified.
"But before I forget. I was going through some portfolios the
other day and I came across a sketch my late husband made for
his portrait. I thought perhaps you might like to have it."

"But how generous of you!" he said. "I'd love to have it some
time."

"Pull the bell for me," she said, "and you shall have it now."

An elderly maid came in, and she was somewhat deaf for she strained with a sideways twist of the head to hear the orders.

"I'm sure she'll bring the wrong thing," Henrietta said resignedly. "She always does. The only problem with servants nowadays is that there are none. And now tell me what made you come."

"I'll be honest," he said, and his fingers went instinctively to his glasses. "I really came to tell you some important news. . . . Sonia's dead."

"Really?" There had been no more than polite inquiry, but the thin lips closed tightly and her look was all at once across the room as if there were things her inner mind had seen.

"She was murdered . . . last night, at Montage Court."

He saw her start at that. Her grey eyes narrowed and her look was full on him.

"She was spending the first day or two of her honeymoon there. More I don't know, except that it was naturally an overwhelming shock for Sidley."

"Naturally."

He seemed to catch an irony in the very evenness of her tone. No passing of time or pathos of circumstance would ever dull the memory of Irene, and there was no need to wonder where Philip got his own tenacity of hates.

"I suppose you haven't run across Sidley much lately?" he said.

"Sidley and I never had much in common," she said. "We speak different languages. I believe he finds my English very old-fashioned, and I've never been able to acquire Yiddish."

He shook his head. "That was not very kind of you—"

A tap at the door and the elderly maid came in again with the sketch. Henrietta made signs for her to leave it on the side table.

"Perfectly amazing! She seems to have brought the right one." She stirred in the chair as if trying to recall what trivialities had been interrupted. "Very good of you indeed, Ludovic, to let me know."

"I don't know," he said lamely. Then he looked up. "Philip about anywhere? I saw him the other day and I rather gathered he was staying here for a time."

"He left this morning at about ten," she said. "He has a new flat, you know. He's taking it over today."

"Still in Bloomsbury?"

"No," she said, and felt on the mantelpiece for a card. "Philip was beginning to find Bloomsbury rather remote. He's now at"—she read—"33 Buttery Walk, Victoria."

"I think perhaps I'll see him there," he said, and got to his feet. "I may be able to save him some bother."

Her eyebrows rose.

"It's the police," he said. "I expect all the family will be asked to throw what light they can on things."

"But Philip," she said. "How very impertinent!"

He smiled dryly. "The police have annoying ideas of the pertinent and the impertinent, that's why I thought I might possibly save the annoyance. They'll certainly want to know—politely enough—where he was last night between eleven and midnight."

"How ridiculous!" She gave a little snort. "He was here, in this house."

He smiled disarmingly. "Then why not tell me all about it and save the annoyance?"

"But what have you to do with it, Ludovic?"

"Well, I happened to be made aware that the police were likely to come here and make inquiries, so naturally I thought at once I could save you considerable annoyance, and shock. Still, you say that Philip was here. That sounds good enough to me."

"Of course he was here," she said. "I retired at ten-thirty, as I always do, and he came up to his room later. His room is next to mine, I should tell you. I heard him at intervals in his room. I'm a very bad sleeper and he has a most peculiar snore. A legacy, poor dear, from his illness of last year." Her eyes suddenly opened. "But something peculiar did happen last night. I remember now it was just about midnight I heard something unusual, and he must have heard it himself. There was no snoring, you see. Then he tapped at my door and asked if I had heard anything. The result was that he went down to investigate. We rather suspected that it was someone after his car. That was at the old garage, you know, over by the side gate."

"And was it car thieves?"

"Philip thought it was. The lock, he said, had been tampered with."

Travers heaved a sigh. "Well, I don't think the police will come bothering you here. Now perhaps I'd better be going. Some time soon perhaps you'll let me come to lunch."

"My dear boy!" She smiled as he helped her from the chair. "But we're forgetting the sketch."

"An admirable likeness!" he said, and held it at a distance. "These modern people may have a slickness but they lack the touch."

That pleased her enormously. Travers followed up the advantage.

"I wonder if you'd let me give you something—not in return, but as a tiny tribute. My brother-in-law has some most delightful spaniel puppies. May I send you one?"

She made a moue of horror. "My dear boy! for myself, of course, I'd love it, but Philip—!" She shrugged her shoulders. "I don't know how he's acquired that aversion to dogs, but they simply make him shriek. Like spiders, you know, and snakes and things. Let me have that drawing wrapped up for you."

"Not at all," Travers said. "I'll put it here, on the back seat, and this rug over it."

She leaned on her stick and watched.

"What a beautiful car! I think people have lost the taste for really beautiful things."

"Some time you must let me come and bring you up to town in it," he said. His hand went out. "Good-by. And thank you for the drawing. And for letting me rush in so suddenly like this."

His hand went out to wave back as the car swung round by the gate, but it was of Philip he was thinking when the open road was reached. So Philip had an alibi, which was a pity, for he had been apt enough for the job if he could have screwed up the pluck. That was the trouble with those writers of horrific plays and Grand Guignol thrillers—they would probably faint at the sight of the blood they splashed so readily about their gory pages.

He smiled to himself then as he remembered that devastating snore. Henrietta had apparently not moved Philip from the room adjoining hers because she found those amazing noises something of a comfort in her sleeping hours. Then he remembered another thing—Philip's spectacles. If he had been the fake ghost—which seemed hopelessly improbable—then the light of the torch on those horn-rims would have made them look like headlights to old Coales.

Yet all the time Travers would keep thinking how great a pity it was that Philip had been eliminated, for last night's weird and tortuous business of murder had been compounded of the very ingredients of which he fashioned those pseudo-medieval tragedies which had made his name. And yet, of course, that was hardly correct as a statement. The Montage Court killing seemed composed not of one drama but of two, which might be entitled *Sonia's Revenge* and *The Montage Ghost*. And on the face of it, they were two unconnected happenings, and therefore not to be solved from one suspect or one set of clues.

As he came to the first of the main suburbs, the posters of the morning papers caught his eye, and he pulled up the car and bought a selection. Practically full of racing news, all of them, but each with its headlines of the murder of Sonia. Nothing however but that bald statement, and the rest all biography and padding, and promise of details in later editions. Then he saw something else: the police anxious to have news of the whereabouts of a man calling himself Doctor Richard Stavangel, lately connected with oil companies in the Middle East. A description followed.

Then he saw another thing, and of somewhat more personal interest, though it was deemed worthy of no more than a quarter-column.

EARL OF DALHOUN
ROMNEY MASTERPIECE DISAPPEARS

The disappearance was evidently the result of a burglary, though again most of the details were either unknown or had been crowded out. Travers remembered well enough the sensation in the saleroom when that picture had fetched twenty thousand guineas, and how later the purchaser, young Lord Wryde, was said to have refused a considerable profit from America. Wryde must have been a fool, thought Travers, to have kept a thing of that value at Carlton Square. Whether he ever got it back or not, it would have been cut from its frame, and that would have meant considerable damage considering the picture's extremely moderate size.

Then as he drew near town, Travers fell to pondering over the reasons that might have made Philip Carne move so suddenly from his old Bloomsbury headquarters to a new flat in—of all places for a highbrow—Victoria! Curious too that the move should have been made on the morning after the Montage murder, and—more curious still—that Carne should never have mentioned it that evening in the club.

But when Travers crossed Westminster Bridge he was grateful that the new flat lay so handy. Buttery Walk proved even more convenient for himself than he could have hoped, though it was a narrow street and somewhat dingy. The number he needed was on the side door of a small second-hand furniture and junk store, closed apparently for the day, but the door opened to a passage at the end of which was a flight of stairs.

Philip Carne opened the door to his knock, and he was looking a most unusual figure in short sleeves and with an apron round his waist. Sweat was on his pale brow and his lank black hair was wispy.

"Morning, Carne," Travers said. "Too busy to spare a minute?"

"Come in, do," Carne said. "But how the devil did you know I was here?"

"I happened to see your mother this morning," Travers said, "and she told me about the change of flat."

"Not a bad place on the whole," Carne said, and moved a chair nearer the dull fire. "Unfortunately I had to take it furnished. Perfectly bloody collection, don't you think?"

Travers smiled. "It is rather terrifying."

"I have my own things, of course." He pointed to the jammed assortment at the end of the long room. "Had them dumped here yesterday. Now I'm trying to straighten things out. Cigarette?"

"Thanks, no," Travers said. "I think I'll try a pipe." He paused over the filling, then looked up. "I have some news for you, by the way, unless you've already heard it."

"Indeed?"

"Soma's dead."

"Dead!" He took off his glasses and blinked. "My dear fellow, you're not serious. You mean, she was killed in a crash, or something?"

Travers shook his head. "Murdered, last night, at Montage Court."

"Good God!" His head was shaking bewilderedly as he hooked the glasses on. "But how on earth did she get there?"

Travers explained, and wondered if by any lucky chance Carne could throw any light.

"I only wish I could." He clicked his tongue. "It's so amazing, and sudden. I mean, you just can't find any words at all." He looked quickly up. "The police any idea who did it?"

"At the moment I'm afraid not."

Carne clicked his tongue again. "My God! it's a bad business. I hadn't much use for Sonia, but this—well, it's hellish, that's all I can say."

Travers was getting to his feet. "Well, I must be pushing on. I just thought perhaps you'd like to know. Oh, by the way, your mother was telling me you'd had trouble down at Severns last night."

"Trouble?" He smiled. "Oh, yes. I mean, there might have been. I didn't sleep any too well. Thought I kept hearing noises—you know the kind of thing. I nearly got up at about half-past eleven only I didn't want to disturb my mother. She's a very light sleeper, you know, and I rather thought she was asleep at the time. Then round about midnight I really decided to get up, and my mother actually confirmed that she'd heard noises too. So I went downstairs, and out, and had a listen, then I pushed off to my garage, and then I thought I heard a car move off just along the lane. I might have been mistaken but I don't think I was. And I found the padlock on the garage door nearly filed through. The local police took it away this morning but they said there weren't any prints."

"You were just in the nick of time apparently," Travers said, and moved off to the door.

"You must have a look at this place now you're here," Carne said. "I had to leave the other, as a matter of fact. They were raising the rent and had a new tenant waiting to move in if I jibbed."

It was quite a good flat, as Travers admitted. Carne was delighted with it himself.

"Too many publishers in Bloomsbury for my liking," he said. "And the people one was forced to meet. I tell you, my dear Travers, I was one perpetual retch. More traffic there too, of course. This is quite a backwater."

Two minutes later Travers had steered the car back to Eccleston Square, and before he moved on to the main traffic he was wondering what move should come next. Patrick Carne would be lunching at one of his clubs, so why not lunch himself? Should he locate Patrick's flat and lunch in the immediate neighbourhood?

But as he drove on towards Victoria Station he faced up to something that was at the back of his mind. Why had Carne of his own accord been so extravagant of reasons for taking the new and leaving the old? Maybe it had been only a desire to talk—to cover the shock, perhaps, of the Sonia news—and yet there had been too much of it. And once more there was the appositeness of the leaving of one flat on the eve of the murder and the taking of a new one the morning after. A queer business altogether, thought Travers, and then with a sudden intuition which he himself knew as ridiculous, he turned the car into Victoria Street with that Bloomsbury flat as objective.

VII
INQUIRY CONTINUED

THAT OLD FLAT of Philip Carne's lay above a publisher's warehouse, and the first thing that struck Travers as strange was that the notice to let should be in its window. Carne had distinctly said that the agents had a tenant ready to step in, but that might have been either exaggeration or the fact that the prospective tenant had failed the agents.

There was a telephone in the warehouse and he obtained permission to ring up the agents from there. A voice informed him that a clerk would be sent along at once with the keys and would be with him in five minutes.

The clerk arrived and his eyebrows lifted at the sight of the Rolls. He had already spent the morning at the flat, making things shipshape after the departure of the last tenant, so he told Travers. Travers declined to give a name. Ample time for that, he said, if he decided to take the flat. From the quick look in the clerk's eye, he knew the worst was being thought—nothing less perhaps than the installing in that nest of some lady of greater charm than virtue.

The clerk unlocked the door and gave the usual flourish.

"Here we are, sir, and though I say it, as nice a place as you'd find anywhere in the neighborhood at twice the rent."

"Furnished, I see," Travers said. "None too gaudily, do you think?"

"That could be arranged, sir, if you wished to install your own."

"Noisy, is it?"

"Well, it is, just a bit, in the day-time," the clerk admitted. "There's a fair amount of noise from below, sir. But at night—well, it's just as quiet as the country."

Travers nodded, his mind already admitting the fact that Carne had a good reason for leaving. And since the secondary lair of a publisher lay beneath him, maybe that accounted for that last satire of his—*Hot from Hell*.

Then Travers took a seat in the corner of the settee while the clerk enlarged on the flat's advantages. Then something thin, apricot in color and rather like a hair, showed itself on Travers's dark brown trousers. As he listened to the eulogies of the clerk his fingers removed it, and at the same time he was aware that many hairs of the same kind were attached to the upholstery of that settee where he sat. Then as he talked himself he idly surveyed one. A hair it was, and the silky hair of a cat.

But the clerk was suggesting a move to the other rooms, and Travers rose. As he walked and talked he was still wondering and thinking. Curious that Carne should have such a horror of dogs and like a cat enough to keep one confined in that flat. An amusing idea presented itself, and he surreptitiously turned a tap in the bathroom basin. A minute later, he was cocking an ear in the main room.

"Pardon me, but do I hear water running?"

The clerk nipped away to investigate. Travers collected a dozen or so of the silky fawn hairs and placed them in an old envelope, and he was at the outer door when the clerk came back. And he was all apologies. It was himself, he now recalled, who must have left that tap running.

"And about the flat, sir? You think you'll like it?"

"I doubt it," Travers said. "In fact, so as to waste no more of your time, I think you'd better forget this visit altogether."

It took another half-hour to reach the confines of Sloane Square and again the telephone directory was consulted for Patrick Carne's precise address. His turned out to be one of a pair of flats—quite refined in character—converted out of a former mews. When Travers came to confront the two doors, he grew confused about the numbers, with no idea which after all was Carne's. The top one probably, he thought, and mounted the steps and knocked at what would be the door at the foot of its stairs.

An elderly man opened the door and he had something of the look of a pianist, for he wore his hair longish and sported a flowing tie.

"I'm sorry," Travers began at once. "I'm afraid I made a mistake. I took this for Mr. Carne's flat."

"The lower one," the man said, made as if to close the door, then opened it wider. Then he gave Travers a close look. "Are you a friend of his?"

Travers hedged. "Not exactly, and yet I suppose I am—in a way."

"H'm!" said the man and gave another look. "It's a pity you aren't a friend of his, so that you could give him some advice."

Travers smiled. "Well, I might manage that."

The man plunged at once into his grievances.

"Then do you tell him that if he doesn't stop kicking up those noises when I'm asleep, he's in for trouble. I've spoken once and now I'll put the matter in other hands."

"What noises are they?" Travers asked sympathetically.

"When he comes in. About half-past eleven usually, and he starts blundering into things. Tight, I should say, most of the time. Then he puts the wireless on and that's blaring away till midnight. I admit he always turns it off then, but that's not good enough. I'm in bed before eleven, as I told him, and if I don't get my sleep I can't get on with my work next day."

"Every night, is this?"

"Well, not every night. Once a week and sometimes oftener."

Travers nodded, then put the quick smiling question.

"But not last night?"

The other glared. "Of course it was last night! Isn't that what I've been trying to tell you? Nearly twelve o'clock it was and down went something with a clatter you could have heard over half the neighborhood. Then the wireless went on." He remembered something far more important. "Then I got knocked up by the police because of a man they thought prowling round. He was supposed to have gone into that bottom flat, so why they had to disturb me I can't think."

"I'm sorry about it all," Travers said. "I expect Mr. Carne will see reason when he thinks it over."

"I'm very grateful to you," the man said. "Might I ask your name?"

"We'd better not let that out," Travers told him mysteriously. "You see, I might not speak to Mr. Carne at all. I might do it through a third party. I'd just as soon you didn't mention it, by the way."

Patrick Carne, he was almost certain, would be at his club, but he knocked at the door of that lower flat, and heard no sound in reply. The Rolls had been left round the corner and as he walked slowly that way his mind was busy over a new problem—the curious story of the long-haired man. For that story seemed fantastic in each of its details. Patrick Carne, coming home from his club at round about half-past eleven. There presumably he had been playing bridge, and for fairly high stakes, with men as expert as himself. Yet he was supposed to come home so tight that he blundered into things and kicked up the devil of a din. Absurd on the face of it. How could a man make a living out of bridge when he was half tight? Bacchus was surely the ally of Venus, not of the goddess of chance.

Then there was that putting on of the wireless, at an hour when crooners were fouling the air. Still, that might be possible. Aside from bridge, what precise backgrounds and soul had Patrick Carne? Maybe that kind of din was mightily to his taste, appealing as it did to those inclined to obvious rhythms and the frankly cheerful or even the maudlin.

But that mention of a call by the police, that seemed somewhat interesting, and on a sudden impulse Travers pulled up the car by a traffic policeman and asked for Divisional Headquarters. There he was lucky enough to find a Detective-Sergeant, which meant a quick identification of himself.

"I think I remember something about it, sir," he told Travers. "If you wait here half a mo., I'll look it up."

He came back with the news that he could have the actual man on hand inside ten minutes. Travers used the wait to ring up his own flat and ask Palmer to have ready a meal in half an hour.

That half-hour was almost up when the constable appeared and his story seemed hardly worth waiting for. He had been in the neighborhood of the flats at about one o'clock when he caught sight of a dark figure moving towards the side or tradesmen's door of the lower flat. When he reached the spot himself there was never a sign, so he looked round for a time, then decided to knock up the occupier. A gentleman—obviously Patrick Carne—had come sleepily to the door.

Carne had heard nothing and seen nothing, since he had been fast asleep, but he allowed the officer to look through the rooms, and, as far as concerned the interest of Travers, that was that. Within two minutes Travers was heading for home and lunch.

By the time the meal was over it was past three o'clock. Travers pondered the next move, then decided to ring up Norris. The conversation was as follows.

Travers. "That you, Norris? Wharton back yet?"

Norris. "Not yet, sir. The last I heard was how he mightn't get here till dark."

Travers. "Any news your end?"

Norris. "Not too much, sir. They didn't find any drug in her. He was all right though."

Travers. "Anything on that towel?"

Norris. "Nothing on that, sir. She made too good a hand of the glass before she wiped it."

Travers. "What drug was it, do you know?"

Norris. "One of the—some sort of group. Wait a minute, sir. I've got it written down somewhere. . . . Here we are, sir. One of the dichloromethanes. Menzies let on they really didn't know what it was, not really. You there, sir?"

Travers. "Yes."

Norris. "Something else from Menzies. She wasn't—well, not everything a husband's got the right to expect. Get me, sir?"

Travers. "I think so. And very chastely put. And that's the lot?"

Norris. "I think so. Oh, about his nibs. You know how you said he'd be when we let him know what she was dishing up for him? Well, you were right. He's been scowling about the place like a bear with a sore head."

Travers. "Absolutely recovered, has he?"

Norris. "Near enough as makes no difference. The Gen—the Super'll be putting him through the hoop when he gets back to-night. What about your end, sir?"

Travers. "Everything negative. Everyone's got an alibi. Cheerio then, Norris. See you somewhere about six o'clock."

So that was that, thought Travers as he hung up the receiver. Sonia, as Norris had put it, was not all that Cordovan might have expected, which disproved a certain rumor that she had been not only heartless but sexless. But the interesting thing would be to know who was the man or men. Suppose it had been Trove, for instance, and he really was still alive. Extraordinary affair, and the disappearance of that chap Stavangel—

A glance at the clock and he was ringing up Rowlandson's, the most likely of Patrick Carne's clubs. Mr. Carne was not in, he was told, but he would certainly be in at 4.30 when there was a committee meeting he was to attend. Travers left it that he would be along himself at 4.15, and if Carne came in earlier he was to be informed.

With almost an hour to wait, Travers treated himself to a change of clothes, then found that cipher copy and cast an exploratory eye over it. The letters were in groups of five, so he tried first *Vorge* and then *Trove* as the key words, after which the last state of the cipher was worse than the first. So he put it away again with the consoling thought that where the Yard experts had failed, a novice like himself could hardly succeed.

A pipe, and it was time to move on again. It was just short of a quarter past four but Patrick Carne had already arrived and was waiting upstairs.

"Hallo, Travers," he said, in that lack-luster voice of his. "I expect you want to talk. Come along in here."

It was a small, empty room, fireless, but not cold. Carne silently drew two chairs together.

"Won't you sit down. It's about Sonia, isn't it?"

"That's it," Travers said, and waited.

"Perfectly horrible business. I don't know when I've had such a shock as when I saw one of those damn newspaper posters with the news scrawled all over it." He shook his head. "I don't seem to be able to think, or anything. Knocked me all of a heap. I suppose it did you too."

"Yes," said Travers. "So damnably sudden. I suppose you can't throw any light on things?"

He shook his head again. "Afraid not. Wish to God I could. I'm not much of a fighter these days but I'd like five minutes with the swine that did it."

"The police'll get him," Travers said, and got to his feet. "Well, I won't keep you from your meeting. I'm pretty busy myself too." Then suddenly he changed his mind. His smile might have been described as roguish. "By the way, I called at your flat, only I didn't—it was the wrong one. Your upstairs neighbor took me for a brother of yours or something and started ladling out good advice. He says you wake up his household of nights. I rather gathered that you came home tight and barged into things and kicked up the very devil of a racket."

"Priceless old fool!" He smiled. "Sorry he bothered you, but he's not quite normal, that chap. I should think I've barged into things twice altogether, and one of them was last night. It's my eyes. I don't see too well in the dark if I haven't switched on."

"But you're not clear yet," Travers said. "There was also a grievance about your turning on the wireless."

"To hell with him," said Carne serenely. "I happen to like a spot of music when I get in. Sort of acts as a soporific with me, you know. A chap gets a bit moody living alone."

They parted on the landing; Carne going along the corridor to his meeting, and Travers downstairs. In the main lobby whom should he run across but Colonel Faujoic.

"God bless my soul! Ludovic Travers!" the Colonel said. He had been at the Yard soon after the war, and after a minor breakdown had never returned. He was a wealthy man but his heart was still in that old job.

"How are you, Colonel? Pretty fit?"

"Can't grumble, Travers; can't grumble. What about tea? I've just got time."

"Good of you," Travers said, "but the fact is, I haven't. I'm just off to the country."

"Ferreting?" said the Colonel, with a lift of the eyebrows.

"Yes" said Travers. "That's the sport of the moment. And by the way, I've been seeing your name pretty frequently nowadays. You're getting quite a loud noise in the bridge world."

"Me? I'm not even a pop-gun," the Colonel said, and followed Travers through the swing doors. "The same car you had in the autumn? I see it is, though."

Travers had been drawing nearer.

"A word for your private ear. It's the Sonia murder we're on at the moment. I wonder if you'd do something that might possibly help?"

The Colonel waved a hand.

"Patrick Carne's her cousin by marriage. Something's often intrigued me. Does he make as much money at bridge as is sometimes supposed?"

"Get in the car," the Colonel said, "and drive me on for a bit. Too risky talking here."

The car crawled on and he began.

"Carne's a damn clever player. I know. I play with him and against him."

"What's his chief asset? Sheer brain?"

The Colonel pursed his lips. "No. I'd say it's his absolute imperturbability. People who don't know him underestimate him, and that's where he makes his money."

"How much?"

"Now you're asking. He's up on balance; I'd be prepared to swear to that, and he has been for years. Tell you what. I'll make a careful inquiry, if that's any good to you."

"That's the trouble," Travers told him. "Still, you know how things are. You may go to a lot of bother and get the information and then it mayn't be worth a damn. Then again it might be something that fits in."

He drew the car up at the curb. The Colonel gave a quick lowering of the eyelid, smiled, and moved off. Travers heaved a sigh and moved the car on again. The evening traffic was dense and it was well after five when he drew in at a quiet roadhouse for tea.

It was a different Montage Court which Travers reached that early evening, and he could tell from the cars that were left what the rush of sightseers must have been during the day. But police were on duty at the gates, and the house itself had a quiet and a peace. In the main hall by the huge open fire Norris sat over his tea.

"Hallo, sir!" he said. "Looks as if you've caught me out."

"I doubt it," Travers said. "If you've had anything like my day it's been a busy one."

"That's what the Super just rung up and said." Norris resumed his meal "He thought he'd be along some time before six."

"Where's Mr. Cordovan?"

Norris nodded back. "In the drawing-room. He's well under observation, only he doesn't know it. You'd like a word with him, sir? Might cheer him up."

Sidley Cordovan looked up from his chair by the fire and merely scowled when Travers walked in. Travers smiled affectionately.

"Well, how are we now? Feeling better? But I can see you are."

The pink had certainly come back to his cheeks, though there was still a remnant of weariness.

"Bit better," he said surlily.

Travers warmed his hands at the fire. Cordovan broke the silence.

"Pretty hellish thing, don't you think so?—if it's true about last night."

"Yes," said Travers, and from his six foot two looked gravely down at Cordovan. "But it's a queer world. And tell me. I don't want to intrude on privacies, but perhaps you'd like to talk to me in semi-confidence. You'll pardon the apparent brutality of the question, but just what was she like with you last night? Say up to the time when you came upstairs."

He grunted. "Stand-offish, same as she always was. Damn superior—you know what I mean. Like an iceberg, that's what she was, till she poured out that drink. I thought there was something fishy about that, even when she asked me to tell Coales to bring the drinks upstairs." He scowled. "Hell of a business for me if it all comes out."

"It won't come out," Travers told him quietly. "That is, if you tell the police unreservedly all you know."

"Dammit! what should I know?"

"Can't say," said Travers.

"Someone ought to be here. Why don't they get the damn business over and finish with it? How long am I going to be kept here?"

"That again depends on yourself," Travers told him. "I've no authority to speak, but I don't see why you shouldn't get away tomorrow morning."

"My God! another night here!"

"Even that will depend on yourself," Travers said. "You come absolutely clean, as they say, and you'll be treated with every consideration."

There was a cough from the door and Norris stepped in.

"Excuse me, gentlemen, but the Super's asking for you, Mr. Travers. He's just come in." He smiled over at Cordovan. "You needn't look impatient, sir. He'll be finished with you long before dinner."

VIII
CLEAR AS MUD

"WHAT A DAY!" said Wharton. "What a day!"

"Been pretty busy?" asked Travers dryly.

"Busy?" He snorted. "I gulped down a half-pint and a sandwich some time in the morning and I haven't had a second for a bite since. How the devil much longer is that fellow Coales going to be over that tea?"

Norris caught Travers's eye and ventured on a quick grimace. Then Coales came into view with the tray and Wharton was all meekness and mildness again.

"Ah! thank you, Coales." Norris waited for the ancient joke and it duly came. "If ever the cops grab you, send for me and I'll stand bail."

"Make yourselves at home," he told the two, "and don't mind me talking and eating at the same time. But about you, Mr. Travers. Anything happened?"

"Never a thing," Travers said. "All sorts of oddments but nothing that's any good. Both the Carnes have alibis."

"Cast-iron?"

"Better than that," Travers said. "Hand-wrought steel."

"Hand-wrought may be home-made," Wharton said, and chuckled at the retort. "Still, I'll take your word for it."

"A court of law is the real test," Travers told him. "Both the Carnes can bring ample evidence to prove they were elsewhere at the vital times. But what about you, George? What did you discover?"

"Not so much as I hoped," Wharton said piously, and Travers knew he was very well pleased. "First I saw the Powers That Be—you know, the people who get things done. They tell me the Austrian authorities are now expecting to find the plane at any moment. Pretty lonely country, wasn't it, where it came down?"

"I suppose it was," Travers said. "But it wasn't exactly that; it was the snow. According to Sonia's story they were forced down among the hill forests in blinding snow. That's why the searching planes could never hope to see a trace. But why the sudden Austrian activity?"

"Not so sudden as all that," Wharton said. "We set them stirring over the Stavangel affair. If Trove was dead, then Stavangel was a liar, and if he was a liar, then he was probably a myth. Which, by the way, looks like being true. That cipher was a fake. All gibberish, the experts say."

"Then why take the trouble to issue that police description and the appeal in this morning's papers?"

"Why?" Between bites be paused to glare.

"We're all human, aren't we? Can't we make mistakes?"

Travers smiled. "When you appeal to my better nature, then I'm dumb. Still, much as I hate to say it, I still think the Stavangel affair was publicity."

"I believe the paper."

"Why shouldn't you?" Travers asked disarmingly. "I say that someone saw a scheme to make money, and on account of the enormous news-interest of the Sonia wedding. He faked himself up as Stavangel—though there mayn't ever have been any such real person—and hoped to get money from the *Evening Record*. Then he lost his nerve and bolted, covering up his tracks with that fake robbery and the cipher message."

"Indeed?" said Wharton, peering over the tops of his anti-quated spectacles. "What do you say then to the fact that Odessa reports there is a Doctor Stavangel, who is black-bearded and has a scar on his wrist?"

"Merely this." Travers was completely unconvinced. "The faker met Stavangel somewhere, or had been acquainted with him, and therefore modelled himself accordingly."

"We'll see," said Wharton laconically. "But you have intui-tions that I respect, so why shouldn't you respect mine? I feel it in my bones that that hotel business was connected with this murder. I can't help it if I feel that way, can I?"

"Certainly not," agreed Travers. "Still, finding that plane ought to clear up most things."

"So would finding the real Stavangel," Wharton admitted. "I must tell you about that Hendon flat, by the way. A bit of bad luck over the maid, Mabel Parker. She was only there the last year; took the place of some old family retainer who'd been with Sonia all her life. But she did say she had instructions to have lunch ready for three people at one o'clock. You've told us that you and Sonia were two—what I couldn't find out was who was the third."

He pushed his plate aside and began wiping his mustache with wide sweeps of his voluminous handkerchief. Travers cut hastily in.

"What else did you find out, George?"

"You'll hear in a minute," Wharton said, checking the papers in the attaché case. "I want to have it all nice and fresh for Cordovan. You two just watch and listen and I'll handle him my own way."

Wharton excelled at interviews and cross-examination. In his time he had himself been questioned publicly and exhaustively by counsel whose names were also front-page news, and it was doubtless from them that he had borrowed much of the histrionics and learned most of the craft. But in any case quite a respectable actor had been lost when Wharton joined the Force. Moreover, from long association, Norris and Travers had learned never to be surprised, though on this particular occasion Norris was hard put to it to keep an immobile face.

"Why, Mr. Cordovan is still here! Surely he might have been allowed to go back to town?"

Norris mumbled something about not quite understanding.

"Well, never mind," Wharton said. "I'm sure he'll forgive us. After all, we might have had to ask him to keep on running down here. And how are you now?" he said. "Feeling your old self again?"

Cordovan, suddenly gracious, admitted he was much better.

"I know," Wharton told him with a sad shake of the head. "These things take some getting over. Still, we shan't be keeping you long now. Just a few simple answers to a few simple questions, and everything in the strictest confidence. We're all men of honour and—I trust—men of goodwill."

Those bletherings over, he re-adjusted his spectacles and made considerable play with the papers in his case.

"Oh, yes," he said. "We must go more fully into the choice of this particular place for the first few days of the honeymoon. Will you tell us all about it? Whose idea it was, and how the suggestion arose?"

Cordovan's lip curled. "I hadn't any say in the matter. It was all done for me."

Wharton waved an encouraging hand. "Well, enlarge on that; do you mind?"

He frowned for a minute in thought. "Well, it started just after the engagement, so I think—"

"Just one moment. The engagement, or the re-engagement?"

Cordovan shot him a look. "Well, the re-engagement, if you want it that way. Just about a month ago, it was, when my uncle was over."

Travers was startled out of silence. "You mean, Sir Raphael was in England?"

"Yes," he said. "I hadn't seen him for three or four years and I didn't even know he was here. You see, Sonia forgot that I was coming to her flat that afternoon, and he was there, and Patrick Carne—I mean, I afterwards knew that. What I happened to overhear was Sonia saying to Patrick, 'There's nothing in his seeing his own uncle.' I thought that was a queer thing and I've thought so since."

"Your idea was that they were keeping your uncle to themselves?"

"Well, yes. Trying to influence him over his will. I mean, that's what I've thought since. It was all most extraordinary really. Sonia said she'd forgotten about my coming, and Patrick said he just happened to call, and when I'd had no more than a dozen words with the old boy, Sonia said he had to be going, and off she went with him. Hustled him off in the most barefaced way. Then she came back and said she was most frightfully sorry but she'd have to cancel our date and would I mind running along and she'd see me next day. It's my belief she simply took the old boy into another room and pretended he'd gone off. Soon as I'd gone, out he popped again."

"I see. And how's this concern the choice of Montage Court for the honeymoon?"

"Well"—he shook his head—"it doesn't, not directly. But she suggested it next day and I connected the two things. I thought she'd obtained permission from my uncle."

"I follow, I follow," said Wharton. Then he leaned forward. "Just how did your uncle strike you? I mean—in strict confidence, of course—there've been all sorts of rumors about his health; well, health of mind."

"I never did take to the old boy," he said. "He never seemed to have much use for me, I don't know why. I know I couldn't give him any points at his game but he couldn't give me any at mine."

"Exactly," said Wharton. "But how did he strike you that afternoon?"

"Not too voluble." The smile was cynical. "He asked how I was and why I didn't come to see him, and I said it was a bit too far. That's all there was to it. I must say he was looking frowstier than I'd ever seen him, and that's saying something. I reckon you could have got about ten bob at a secondhand dealer's for every stitch he had on."

"Ah, well," said Wharton. "The old must have their little eccentricities. But to revert to the honeymoon. Did you ever hear any precise reasons why you should come here at all? I've got a hazy idea you would have preferred to go straight to Egypt."

Cordovan shrugged his shoulders. "You know what it is. There was some argument, then I gave way. Sonia thought it would be romantic to come here. What the devil she meant by romantic, I don't know."

"Well, we'll leave that," Wharton said, "and come to something very personal. You mustn't be offended, Mr. Cordovan, because you can't always see just what's at the back of our minds. Take Maurice Trove, for instance. You didn't like him."

Cordovan shot another look, then wriggled in his chair.

"I liked Maurice all right. The thing was she'd got her name connected with his and I told her I expected the acquaintance or whatever it was, to drop. She did as she liked and—very well, then, I broke the engagement off."

"And after?"

"Well"—he smiled somewhat foolishly—"you've been silly about a woman, haven't you?"

"I expect I have," admitted Wharton. "To cut the tale short, you wanted her and you were prepared to take her back if she was agreeable." He made a wry face. "Which brings us to the twenty-five thousand pounds."

Cordovan's mouth gaped.

"That was easy," Wharton told him. "Solicitors bank every source of information open to us. But why the huge sum of twenty-five thousand?"

"That's easily explained. She didn't want any proper marriage settlement. All she insisted on, before she'd renew the engagement, was the gift of—well, she wanted more than that, but we agreed on twenty-five thousand. Her idea was to pay off her debts and have something in hand of her own, out of my control."

"I'm satisfied," Wharton said, and closed the attaché case with a snap. "Anybody else got anything to ask?"

"One question," said Travers. "Were you convinced she was really in love with you when you renewed that engagement?"

He frowned. "What do you think I am? Do you think I'd have married her if I hadn't thought she was as keen as I was?"

Travers nodded. Norris shook his head. Wharton got to his feet.

"One or two things have arisen out of this conversation that may need further advice from you, Mr. Cordovan, so perhaps we'd better fix tomorrow morning for your going. If you prefer it I've no doubt Coales would rig you up a bed down here. The formal inquest is tomorrow, by the way. You, of course, will not be needed."

He nodded, smiled benevolently and made off with the two at his heels. As soon as the door closed he was making for the hall telephone. Travers and Norris went back to the fire and waited.

It was ten minutes before Wharton came over.

"Just checked up with that solicitor of Sir Raphael's. He hadn't the faintest idea Sir Raphael had been in England."

"If you don't mind me saying so, sir," Norris told him, "I didn't see just where we were getting to just now. Were you trying to fasten anything on him?"

"Let's get round this fire," Wharton said, "then we'll see. I don't know how it struck Mr. Travers but I think we're making headway. Wait a moment and I'll show you."

He consulted his notebook, made another entry or two and then was ready.

"Here's the sequence, and if you disagree, then you can stop me. Mr. Travers was right about her marrying him for revenge. She intended the whole thing to be a swindle, and that's why she took cash down, so that when she'd made a laughing-stock out of him and forced a separation, she'd not only have the laugh on him but the ready cash as well." He shrugged his shoulders. "But we've known most of that for some hours. What emerged tonight was the fact that she absolutely forced this place on him for the scene of the swindle, and she began that forcing a *month or more* ago." He peered at them over his spectacle tops. "Well, do you get me?"

Travers was polishing his glasses. "I don't know. But are you wondering if the *whole scheme* was cut and dried then?"

Wharton raised excited hands. "The very thing! Did she have it all worked out in detail or was it made up during the course of the last month as she went along? And if so, did she work it out alone? If she didn't, who helped her?"

"The one she'd been carrying on with," Norris said.

"That leaves us in the dark as much as ever," Wharton told them. "According to Mabel, the maid, men never came to the flat, except on the occasion of that family gathering Cordovan told us about. Indeed, according to Mabel, she hadn't any use for men."

"About Sonia's having the brain to work everything out," Travers said. "It was on the tip of my tongue to say she couldn't; then the more I thought the less I was certain. She never talked about herself or her plans. She always gave one the idea of being indifferent and inscrutable, but she was so supremely reticent and assured that you couldn't help feeling what an amazing brain she must have. An illusion, perhaps, like the one that silent men must necessarily be strong."

"Well, I've a hunch that she worked things out with somebody," Wharton said. "That somebody was the man who was going to be Cordovan's successor ; the man—as Norris says—she'd been carrying on with, and"—he leaned forward—"the man who was to be the third with you at lunch, Mr. Travers, and enjoy the laugh she'd promised you."

"I like that," Travers said. "I like the way it holds together. The trouble is it leaves us still in the dark—unless we can find some other way to inquire what man or men she did associate with during the last month."

"What about that Patrick Carne?"

"Yes," said Travers slowly, and then recalled that gossip he had overheard about Sonia and Philip.

"The two Carnes," said Wharton. "Well, now I'll tell you something. Sonia left a will, dated a fortnight ago and all in order. I'd say that roughly she'd leave about eighteen thousand pounds, and whom do you think she's left it to?" He watched the shaking of heads. "Well, she's left it to Henrietta Carne!"

"All of it?"

Wharton nodded. "Mind you, if it was a sort of expiation for killing the daughter, then it was a pretty decent thing to do. But we're suspicious blokes. It might look to us as if leaving it to the mother was only a very shrewd way of leaving it to the sons—and without attracting attention!" He leaned back triumphantly. "And now tell me all about the alibis."

Travers began with Philip Carne's, prefixing the whole with the remark that the day had revealed a series of queer happenings but never a spot of blood.

"There's another curious thing," Wharton said. "That place Severns is only fifteen or twenty minutes from here. I suppose Lewis has unearthed nothing, Norris?"

Norris smiled wryly. "It's a good secondary road, sir, and everybody heard cars. And it's been dry for days, so if a car stood on the grass or anywhere, there wouldn't be any marks."

"Well, his alibi sounds good enough to me," Wharton said. "It's endorsed by his mother, and whether it's phony or not that's good enough for a jury. What about the other Carne?"

"Before I go on to that," Travers said, "I'd like to ask a question. When you were at Sonia's flat, I suppose you didn't happen to find out if she kept a cat or cats?"

Wharton pursed his lips. Travers added more explanation.

"You might do worse than call up yourself and find out," Wharton said. "It might have been her cat he was keeping. A bit far-fetched, but you never know."

Travers gave a full account of Patrick Carne. Wharton made only one comment but it showed a shrewd observation.

"Well, as far as I can see, you were told only one lie."

Travers stared. "By whom?"

"By your pianist friend. He said Carne was always sensible or thoughtful enough to turn off the wireless at midnight. Wasn't that it?"

"Yes."

Wharton got to his feet. "Well, Carne didn't or doesn't turn it off. It turns itself off automatically at midnight. The B.B.C. close down then, except on Sundays, when it's earlier; unless, of course, they hold yet another little religious service of their own for the staff and charwoman."

Norris caught Travers's eye and grimaced. When the General was bitter, then his brain was always working.

"One little thing," Wharton was going on. "Something occurred to me today. Tell me about Carne the writer. What does he write?"

"Well"—he smiled—"I may have to talk like a literary gent, but he writes satires. The whole world is always divided into two classes for Philip Carne—friends and despicable enemies. On one side is Carne himself and those with whom he happens at the moment to be in accord, and on the other all the rest of the world. He's written very sarcastically about publishers, critics, the stage, the B.B.C., and everybody with whom he's had any disagreement. His last work—*Hot from Hell*—described a delightful reunion of the whole boiling. I loved it."

"Make money, does he?"

"Enough to jog along on," Travers said. "We all buy his poems because we expect each new one simply must include ourselves."

"Bit above my head," Wharton said. "What occurred to me today was that I'd heard or seen his name somewhere. Wasn't

he the chap who wrote that awful play that brought all that pro-
test to the B.B.C.?"

Travers smiled. *"The Paralytic,* the year's radio flesh-creep-
er. Cleverest thing they've ever put on, but what a long-drawn
horror."

"Scandalous!" Wharton said, in his Mr. Growser manner.
"Never ought to have been allowed." He glared round at nothing
in particular, heaved a sigh, and then was his milder self again.

"It mayn't be midnight, but it's dark. Why not have a look
upstairs and get what Mr. Travers calls the atmosphere?"

But self-consciousness was the main foe to that precon-
ceived and wholly artificial mood. Travers found neither eeri-
ness nor inspiration. The house might seem incredibly old, and,
in the dim occasional light, incredibly beautiful and redolent of
romance, but no absorption of its atmosphere brought nearer
a solving. Wharton put the position aptly when he switched on
the gallery lights.

"Well, the dark isn't telling me very much. What about a little light? And we'll try her bedroom."

Norris unlocked the door. On the table where the body had
been were now all the clues that might have a possible bearing:
tray, decanter and glasses, and all the more grisly array including the rope. It was the sight of the chair that gave Travers a
sudden idea.

"George, there's something we've missed. Would you mind
lending me your glass and showing me where the scratch-marks
are on this chair?"

He had a look, then shook his head.

"Very faint, aren't they?"

Wharton grunted. "Of course they're faint. They wouldn't
have been there at all if the person who was standing on it
hadn't wriggled about to keep his balance. And there're two of
them, aren't there? One for each foot?"

"I'm not so sure they are foot-marks," Travers said. "But if
they are, then who made them?"

"Why—" He stopped. "I get you. The ghost didn't make them because he was in stockinged feet."

"Exactly! Therefore it wasn't the ghost who adjusted the rope to the beam."

"Then it might have been Cordovan after all!" That was Norris. Travers shrugged his shoulders.

"Either Cordovan or—his wife. As far as we know, they're the only two left."

Wharton was clicking his tongue exasperatedly. "You mean to say we've got to begin all over again? Assume that Cordovan was shamming after all?"

Travers shook his head. "Don't ask me, George. But on the face of it, it looks remarkably like it."

Wharton raised hands to heaven. "Well, you can do what you like, I'm doing no more thinking for a bit. I've done so much today I'm like a man who's had twenty-four hours at chess."

"What about tomorrow?" Travers asked.

"Norris'll have the inquest. I shall be calling on Mrs. Carne."

Travers was all at once whipping off his glasses. A quick polish and he was replacing them almost sheepishly.

"I've just had the queerest idea. Do you realize that Mrs. Carne is the only one of the three people I saw who hasn't any alibi?"

"But—"

"I know," Travers went on. "She's not the type, you were going to say. Still, there's the fact. She says she heard Philip snoring and then moving about, *but he didn't say he heard her.* He heard suspicious noises *outside.*"

"What about the time? Just after midnight, wasn't it? That wouldn't have given time to have got back from here."

"Round about is very vague," Travers said. "We don't know if Coales's alarm was right, but if it was, even then he saw the ghost well before midnight. Therefore the ghost might have been back at Severns at ten or a quarter past. Putting back the car might have been the noise that Philip heard."

Wharton shrugged his shoulders but rather too elaborately.

"Well, I'm seeing her in the morning."

"Just a minute," said Travers. "You announced that before I mentioned her alibi. What was in your mind, George?"

Wharton smiled dryly. "Just a friendly call—that's all. A word or two of congratulation on having come into a tidy little sum of money."

He moved off to the door. Travers smiled. Norris caught his eye and gave what was remarkably like a wink.

IX
DOUBLE TEAM

TRAVERS WOKE next morning after the soundest night he had known for years. Over night his mind and body had both been tired, but now his mind was uncannily clear.

"Have those photographs come?" was the first thing he asked Palmer.

"They came last night, sir," Palmer said. "Five minutes after you were in bed, sir, but I didn't want to disturb you."

Travers had a look at them—four photographs of Sonia, obtained from the office of the *Record*, and all in costumes other than the Cossack one. What he was proposing was to make two series of inquiries. If men had never been at Sonia's flat, that was no reason why she should never have been at theirs, and so the pianist was going to be shown a photograph. As for Philip's old flat at Bloomsbury, the inquiries there would have to be general, and precisely how he would ultimately set about them, he had not as yet determined.

The whole purport of the inquiries, as he told himself, was an attack on the alibis of Patrick Carne and his brother, while Wharton, who had never met her, was leading his own particular attack on Henrietta Carne. Alibis might be cast-iron and unshakeable, but Wharton and he had tackled such before. Not a direct attack—that would be folly. The method, as experience had shown, was not the frontal attack but a mining and sapping, and a nudging in from the rear or side. An alibi claimed that a suspect could not have been at a certain place at a certain time, and it was generally substantiated by plausible proof that he was elsewhere. The thing to do then was not to worry about that *elsewhere*. Ignore that claim entirely, and let the concentration be on the amassing of a heap of circumstance to show that on the other hand he must have been at that vital time—he, and no other man—at the one spot at which the police wanted him.

With traffic as it was, the Underground was quicker than the Rolls, and soon after nine o'clock Travers was in the neighborhood of Sonia's flat. Then ahead of him he caught sight of a lean, active figure, black-haired and upright, and he quickened his own steps.

"What are you doing here at this hour, Lewis?" Lewis stared, then grinned. "You startled me, sir. And what are you doing, sir?"

"Going to a certain flat," Travers said. "You're merely looking for the number."

"You're right, air." He grinned again, then gave a look of humorous inquiry. "Nothing to do with a cat, I suppose, sir?"

Travers smiled. "Now I remember. I believe we rather left it in the air—the cat, that is. So you're inquiring about the cat. Which reminds me. While you're questioning the maid, ask her if she ever had to ring up any numbers she remembers. There's just a chance."

So Travers left Lewis at the flat entrance and waited in a nearby second-hand bookshop. But he was glad he had seen that flat, if only from the outside. Quite a palatial affair, and it set at rest something that had worried him: why a man like Sir Raphael Breye should have come to a flat—that is to say, the flat of one's ordinary conception—when one of his importance, wealth and reputation should have been at the Ritz or Carlton. Perhaps also Sir Raphael had come there to avoid publicity, for doubtless if they had known of the visit, the reporters would have been after him in a horde.

It was half an hour before Lewis appeared again, and he had a wry face.

"A bit slow in the uptake, that one, sir. First she said her mistress liked cats and then she couldn't tell me why she said it. Then she said she liked dogs and didn't know why she said that either."

"They've never actually ever kept a cat there?"

"Never," Lewis said. "Or a dog either. And she never had to call anybody on the phone." He let out a breath. "So much for that then, sir. And now what?"

"Well," Travers said, "are you in any great hurry?"

"So long as I get back to Montage at one, that'll do me all right, sir. Why, got something on?"

Travers showed the photographs and explained the scheme. Lewis was willing enough to tackle the neighborhood of the Bloomsbury flat while Travers went to Sloane Square. Travers, who had the quicker job, proposed a meeting outside the British Museum at eleven.

Travers made his way to Sloane Square, and what he was to say to Patrick Carne's neighbor he had no precise idea. But the pianist-looking gentleman opened the door once more and the words duly came.

"Good morning. I thought you might like to know that I had a word with a certain person, and I believe you'll not be troubled again."

Thank you, thank you," he said. "It makes a difference to me, you know, being a busy man. By the way, I don't know if you came here thinking to see him, but he's gone away."

No one could have been more surprised than Travers.

"Went by a taxi, just before eight. Had a big bag with him too."

"I wonder he didn't tell me," Travers said. "I've never known him go away before; have you?"

"Oh, yes," he said, "and glad to see the back of him sometimes. I've known him be away twice in a month, and then perhaps he wouldn't be away for two months."

Travers gave a Whartonian grunt. "It's a bit awkward for me this time. Went by taxi, you say." He shook his head. "I wonder if I could find out where."

"The driver was a big man with a fat face and walrus mustache, if that's any help."

Travers nodded. "Thanks very much but I don't think it matters. I expect he'll be back in a day or two."

There was a cab rank at the head of Morford Street and it occurred to him to try it. If Patrick Carne had skipped the country, the sooner Wharton was made aware of it, the better. Three taxis were still in the rank and he approached the driver of the first.

"Is there by any chance a driver here who's a big, fat man with a walrus mustache?"

The driver laid aside his racing news and took a squint round the window.

"Joe Pearce, sir. Just coming in."

A shilling changed hands and Travers moved along the line. Pearce made no bones about telling all he knew.

"Yes, sir, I called for the gent as arranged with him last night and took him to Meadowfield, and come straight back."

"Meadowfield? That's the very devil of a way, isn't it?"

"Matter of sixteen mile, sir. Cushy, this time of morning. Dropped him at the Dragonflies, sir, and then hopped it."

"What's the Dragonflies? A pub?"

"Blimey, no, sir. One o' them Flying Clubs, sir; one of the biggest there is. I've often driven gents out there—ladies too."

A half-crown changed hands, and a despondent Travers made for the Underground. But the despondencies had not yet taken shape and were still only a vague uneasiness, when he caught sight of the telephone booths and on a sudden impulse decided to ring up the Dragonflies and try a bluff.

It was ten minutes before he could ascertain the number, and when a voice answered his call, it was the voice apparently of one without authority, but capable of obtaining the information.

"What name shall I say, sir?"

Travers thought quickly. "Martin Chambers—Sir Martin Chambers."

Good policy to give one's self a handle, he thought, and smiled wryly all the same. Then almost at once a brisk voice was speaking.

"Sir Martin Chambers? . . . Oh, about your inquiry, Sir Martin. I'm afraid you're too late for Mr. Carne. He left well over an hour ago for Paris."

"Most awkward," Travers said, in that same throaty voice of disguise. "I didn't even know he was one of your members."

"One of our oldest members," he was told reprovingly, and in the tone there also seemed to the guilty conscience of Travers to be something of suspicion, and at once he hung up.

He stood for a minute or two outside the kiosk, wondering what move would be best. Carne was certainly a dark horse. One of the earliest members of a Flying Club, and flying, at that very moment, to Paris. Then Travers saw two things, and neither decreased his uneasiness. Flying interests, and nothing else, were most likely the bond between Patrick Carne and Sonia; and that visit to Paris meant no more than that Paris was a port of call on the longer trip to the South, where he was personally giving Sir Raphael Breye an account of the tragedy.

Yet there was a chance that that latter might be wrong and that he was bolting from justice after all. So Travers entered the kiosk again, and this time rang Rowlandson's Club and asked for Mr. Patrick Carne.

"What name, sir, please?"

"Palmer, Geoffrey Palmer."

"Hold the line a minute, sir."

Travers held and waited. A refresher was needed before the information came.

"Mr. Carne is not in the Club at the moment, sir. The impression is that he is away for a day or two, sir."

"Any idea when he'll be back?"

"By Monday afternoon at the latest, sir. He's representing the Club against the Chippendale in the Smythe-Parkinson Cup. Would you like to leave a message, sir?"

"Thanks, but it doesn't matter," Travers said, and replaced the receiver.

Back by Monday afternoon, which certainly didn't look like skipping the country; unless, of course, the arrangement to return was nothing but a blind. And then Travers realized that in the excitement he had forgotten the main object of his call on Carne's neighbor, so with a glance at his watch he retraced his steps. The pianist gentleman showed no particular surprise at the sight of him.

"So sorry to bother you again," Travers said, "but was a lady in the taxi?"

"Not that I saw," he was told.

"She ought to have been," Travers said excitedly. "I remembered just after I left. I've got her photograph here if you'd care to have a look at it." He smiled. "What's your name, by the way, if you don't mind my asking?"

"My name?" He felt in his breast pocket and produced a card. Travers read the name of Henry Lidget, M.A. (Lon.), and noted what seemed a miniature prospectus for the Sloane Correspondence Course of Modern Languages. Meanwhile Lidget was studying the photographs.

"I still don't think there was anyone in the taxi," he said, and then scrutinised the photographs again. "How tall would this lady be?"

"Medium height," Travers said, "and slim,"

He frowned "I actually saw a lady let herself in one evening, when Mr. Carne was out. Then the wireless went on soon after, and I thought I heard voices. One was a man's, so I thought he'd come back again."

"She'd surely never come here," Travers said. "What time was it? Do you remember?"

"About nine o'clock. And I can tell you the date. It was a Saturday, March the—let me see—the twentieth. That was it—the twentieth. I thought I heard a paper boy and my wireless was out of order so I came to the door to buy a paper."

Travers nodded. "And that's the only time she's been here?"

"Well, the only time I've actually seen her. I did hear the wireless one other night when I thought Mr. Carne was out. About a week ago, that'd be."

Travers nodded even more mysteriously as he took back the photographs.

"I understand. You couldn't tell me, of course, if she was slim in build?"

"She wasn't what you'd call big," he said. "It may have been how she looked when her face turned towards that light there but she struck me as being very pale."

"Well, I'm much obliged to you," Travers said. "I'll be even more grateful if you'll keep all this to yourself."

Lidget gave him a shrewd look. "A divorce court business?"

Travers shook a dubious head. "That'd be telling. Form your own opinions, of course, but keep everything under your hat."

A nod, and a smile of thanks, and he was moving on again. Carne, he thought again, was indeed a dark horse and might have women of all sorts at his flat, and yet the mention of a pale face seemed almost an identification of Sonia. And yet why should she not come to his flat?

Then another idea came to him and yet once more he made for that telephone kiosk and rang up Rowlandson's. This time he pitched his voice high with an accent that might have been called hee-haw. What he wanted to know was if Rowlandson's had been playing any other Club on the night of the twentieth of March. The reply was that they were playing the Hogarth in the London Duplicates.

"Could you tell me your team?" Travers said.

"Just a minute," he was told. "Yes, here we are. P. Carne, H. J. Laurimere, Lord Wryde and the Hon. Stuart McGaine. Who are you, by the way?"

"I represent the new American Branch of the Contract Bridge Guild," Travers said uublushingly.

"Never heard of it"

"You will," Travers told him confidently. "The match, I take it, was an evening one?"

"There was an afternoon session and an evening one," the voice said. "Three to six-thirty and eight to eleven-thirty."

The voice seemed to have been acquiring a disrespect and an incredulity, and once more Travers hastily replaced the receiver. And he was even more mystified. Unless the proprietor of the Sloane school of languages was confused in his dates, then whoever had been with the lady in the flat, it had not been Patrick Carne.

It was after eleven when Travers arrived outside the British Museum but no sooner did he halt and look round than a seedy-looking individual came up to him, holding what appeared to be a note.

"Mr. Travers, sir?"

"Yes," said Travers and took the note. It was from Lewis. Would Mr. Travers come to 19, Ballad Court, Soho, as soon as he could. Travers handed over a tip and strode off west by Tonnage Lane. His objective turned out to be the office of Turner and Glide, Private Inquiry Agents, and Lewis was waiting just inside the passage.

"This way, sir," he said. "I don't know what it amounts to but I've got something for you."

Travers was ushered into a scantily furnished cubby-hole where two men were waiting. One was obviously an ex-policeman.

"Mr. Fred Horless, sir," Lewis said. "Used to be in the old 'O' Division, sir."

Travers shook hands with him and with a colorless gentleman of the name of Trim. Lewis explained. He had been going past the Museum when he ran into Horless and, birds of a feather as they were, they had talked shop. Horless was surprised to hear that Lewis was making inquiries within a stone's-throw of the spot where a colleague of his had also recently been making inquiries to do with certain Divorce Court proceedings. Trim was the man and they had returned in search of him, leaving a note to be delivered to Travers.

"How can Mr. Trim help us?" Travers said.

"You tell him, Jim," Lewis said.

Trim said he had been planted in a flat dead opposite that of Philip Carne and his job was to watch who entered the house of a certain party, and take notes of times. He had therefore had the door to Carne's flat beneath his eye and he had never seen a lady enter or leave during the three weeks he had been on the job, which had ended three days ago. But what he had seen almost every night, though by the dimmish light of the street lamp, was Philip Carne leaving his flat with something in his arms which might certainly have been a cat.

Travers made a wry face. "What was he doing? Taking it out for exercise? Or to be cleaned, or what?"

"If it was a valuable cat, sir," Trim said, "he wouldn't trust it loose, especially if it was a she."

"A queer business," Travers said, and frowned.

"But I suppose he sometimes went out without the cat?"

There Trim had to explain the position. He believed so but could not be sure. He was indeed almost certain but could not swear to it. His eyes had been on his main job and the affair of the cat had only stuck in his mind because firstly it was something regular and to be looked for, and secondly it was unusual. And, much as he regretted it, he could give no dates.

Two more tips were given and then at the last moment Travers had another idea. Life had no greater thrill than those problems of detection in the solving of which he was allowed— which was how he would have put it—to lend a hand, and he was prepared to pay for the privilege, and in any case the sums he from time to time expended were shamedly trifling to one of his means. Now he was proposing to save Wharton time and take a short cut.

"This is a pretty good firm?" he asked Lewis.

"One of the most reliable there is," Lewis told him.

So Travers saw one of the principals and gave his instructions. It was to be a kind of rush order. Within as short a time as possible he wished to know whose plane it was in which Patrick Carne had flown that morning to Paris; whether he had gone on from there, and how and to what destination.

He admitted that quick results might be expensive but he was prepared to pay.

Lewis was still waiting outside and the two adjourned for a quick coffee. Travers wrote a summary of the morning's discoveries for Lewis to give to Wharton.

"I don't like the look of that Patrick Carne business," Lewis said. "It looks to me as if he's in it up to the neck, and he got the wind up and hopped it." Then he too thought of something. "But where's this cat come in, sir, that there's all this fuss about?"

Travers blushed faintly. "I think perhaps I'd rather you didn't mention the cat. That was one of my hunches that seems to have gone wrong."

"Just a minute, sir." He thought for a moment. "He's in new rooms now—Philip Carne I mean, sir, and you went there. Did you see the cat there? What I mean is, if it was a valuable cat he'd have taken it with him."

"You're right," Travers said. "If it'd been there he'd have been bound to exhibit it A queer business, as you say." Then he shook his head. "Still, I've magnified trifles before and wasted time over them. I still prefer you shouldn't say any more than you can help to Superintendent Wharton."

As Travers let himself in, he heard the sound of the wireless from the kitchen, and Palmer at once came in and explained.

"I hope the noise wont disturb you, sir, but there's a talk I would like to listen to, sir. It's a series, sir, and this is the fourth."

Travers smiled. "Why shouldn't I listen to it myself?"

Palmer frowned slightly. "I'm afraid you wouldn't care for it much, sir. It's a cookery series, sir. This one is about omelettes."

Travers smiled once more and waved him back to the kitchen. But during lunch he remembered that shrewd remark of Wharton's, about the man Lidget's false impression that Patrick Carne had turned off the wireless in his flat. A queer mind, George Wharton's, with all sorts of out-of-the-way information ready for the tap.

"About the wireless," Travers asked Palmer. "What's the usual way of turning off an electrically operated set like your own? Do you switch off the actual set or turn off the power switch?"

"The power switch, sir," Palmer said. "You see, sir, there might be complications if the current were left running."

"Of course," said Travers, and then Palmer gave a little cough.

"The arrangements for this afternoon or evening, sir. Have you made up your mind, sir?"

"Not yet," Travers said. "I'm expecting a rather important message and when that comes, then we'll see."

It had been his custom for years to go down on a Friday evening to his sister's place in Sussex, and that week-end he was anxious not to delay the visit till the Saturday, for there was the little matter of his brother-in-law's birthday. So he stayed in the flat that afternoon and busied himself with drafting the first outlines of his new book. Then at about four-thirty a call came from the Detective Agency.

Their information was complete. Mr. Patrick Carne had gone to Paris in company with a friend of his whose plane it was, and the friend had since returned. At Paris, Carne had taken the Marseilles plane, which had arrived on time.

Travers was pleased with that, confirming as it did his original suspicion that Carne was bound for St Peranne to give Sir Raphael Breye first-hand news of the Sonia tragedy, and then, no sooner had he replaced the receiver than the bell was going again. This time it was Wharton.

"I've been trying to get you," he said, "but the line was engaged."

He sounded rather short-tempered, and Travers gave him a placatory synopsis of the news about Patrick Carne. Wharton grunted, made no comment, and changed the subject.

"You coming this way as usual tonight?"

"I can come that way," Travers said, smiling at Wharton's easy dismissal of a detour of twenty miles and more.

"Good!" he said. "You'll find me at Montage Court."

"Any special news from your end?" Travers cut in hastily.

"Nothing much," Wharton said, and then gave what sounded like a chuckle. "Your friend Stavangel—the real Stavangel—has been picked up in Persia."

"That's not too far from Odessa," Travers reminded him.

"Odessa, my foot!" Wharton said. "He's never been in Odessa in his life, he says. But he's black-bearded and has a scar down his wrist."

"Does he ever come to England?"

"He's a naturalized Dane," Wharton said, "and spends most of his time here. That's where he and our friend X must have got acquainted."

X
WHARTON MEETS HIS MATCH

THOUGH GEORGE WHARTON let out very little that was likely to give away his own discomfiture, Travers gathered from the manner in which he told of his interview with Henrietta Carne that the General had more than met his match. Which was a noteworthy event.

Wharton always prided himself on his way with women, and though he was rarely one to boast he would at least show such obvious and anticipatory satisfaction at the prospect of questioning such suspects or witnesses, that it was more than plain that he regarded them as sponges apt for the squeezing. Travers had been present at many an interview and had observed with a series of inward chuckles the masterly displays which Wharton had produced: the little references to himself as a family man, the ingratiations, the compliments, the sympathies and the cajolings. In fact he would have given a fiver at the least for a full and official recording of the interview which Wharton had had that morning with the mistress of Severns.

But Travers was never likely to hear just what had transpired, though there was much reading that could be done between Wharton's lines. According to Wharton, she had pretended a deliberate ignorance of the law that had been not unmixed with contempt. What had happened was this.

Wharton had sent in his card by the deaf and elderly maid, and had awaited Henrietta in the drawing-room. Then she had come in, leaning somewhat heavily on her stick, and had given him a look that went clean through him and yet somehow over him.

"Good morning. You have come about the insurance of the maids. Such a nuisance, those stamps, don't you think?"

"I'm afraid not," Wharton began, with one of his most ingratiating smiles.

"The electricity then."

"It's on the card," said Wharton, the least bit ruffled. "Superintendent Wharton of Scotland Yard."

"But one has so many superintendents," she said, and, reflectively: "Scotland Yard. Isn't that where they keep lost property?"

Then there was a something at the very end of the interview that effectively queered the inquisitorial pitch and cut short Wharton's never-failing climax of the farewell.

"A real homely room, Mrs. Carne," he said as he rose to go. "If I may say so, all it needs to give a look of perfect comfort is a real nice cat asleep on that hearthrug."

She looked at him as if he were some queer species.

"Yes," babbled Wharton. "I always think a cat gives the finishing touch to a room—either a cat or a dog."

"Indeed?" she said, then gave a sideways, reminiscent tilt of the head. "My poor dear sister kept dogs. Griffons. The hairy kind, you know. So extremely thoughtless of her. One was always mistaking them for her husband."

So much for the unrecorded episodes. What Wharton said, and with some vehemence, was that he'd have given a week's pay to have slapped the old hag's face.

"Did I say she wasn't the type?" he challenged Travers. "If I did, then may heaven forgive me. She's as hard as nails, that one. I'll bet she'd stand at nothing."

"What did she say when you congratulated her on the legacy?" Travers asked maliciously.

"Asked if I'd come to discuss her private affairs," Wharton said bitterly. "You couldn't talk to the woman. There she sat, looking as if she was some damn duchess and I was a blasted tradesman who'd been sanding the sugar." He smiled grimly. "Still, I told her a thing or two. You ought to have seen the look on her face when I let her know that it might be within my province to ask her to come to the Yard."

"But it isn't within your province," said Travers.

"She didn't know that, did she?" He glared.

"And for heaven's sake, don't you start being awkward. I've had all the awkwardness I can stand for one day." Another grim smile. "Not that I'm without hopes of getting something of my own back."

"Her alibi?" said Travers with a lift of the eyebrows.

"Yes," said Wharton. "There were two or three things I put together and they seemed to fit. Take motive, for instance. Has she any feelings at all—I mean, does she dote on those sons of hers?"

"I can't speak for Patrick," Travers said, "but I think she rather dotes on Philip."

"Well, that's one thing," Wharton said. "If the Sonia woman married Cordovan, whose family I rather gathered she disliked very much, there'd have been children—for all we know, I mean—to share Uncle Raphael's fortune."

"He's worth a million if he's worth a penny," Travers said. "There'd have been plenty to go round."

"Well then, what about that daughter who was killed?"

"She could have murdered Sonia a dozen times for that. Why put it off till now?"

"I tell you there's something fishy," Wharton said. "She called here recently, didn't Coales say so? Said it was a personal call. Why shouldn't she have come here to get the lie of the land sort of photographed on her mind?" Then his look became positively ghoulish. "And just one little thing that seems to have escaped everybody's notice—our friend X, the murderer, limped in order to be the ghost. *She needn't have pretended*; she had to limp!"

"True enough," Travers said. "But she didn't have to flash a torch in her own face."

"Oh, yes," said Wharton confidently, and then made a gracious admission. "Mind you, this is all theory. But I say that she'd have flashed the torch to focus Coales's attention on her face, and she disguised her face either with her hand or by thrusting out her jaw. And the reason why she would draw attention to the upper part of her was that she knew she had to distract attention, and keep his eyes off the lower part of her—*the part that was wearing skirts!*" He paused for his climax. "Maybe she never intended to be taken for a ghost at all. That was pure luck."

"Clever, George, clever." He shook his head. "But even if she did all you say, then she's got you stone cold. Is anything more certain than that Philip would go into the witness box and swear that his mother was at Severns at the vital time?" He shook his head again. "Even if her alibi is a bit tottery at the moment, you can bet your life she'd have Philip primed when the time came."

"I know, I know," said Wharton testily. "But listen to this. That little garage of hers is nice and handy for the house. I don't know if you're aware of it, but there's a door that goes into it straight from the morning-room, so that she needn't go out of doors at all. And do you know the exact slope of the land?"

"Can't say I do," admitted Travers.

"Well, I'll tell you. From within three hundred yards of the house, the road and the drive slope downwards. A car stopped there would run itself home with the engine not running." He wagged an admonitory finger. "Now recall something. Philip admitted he heard a noise that might have been a car in the neighborhood of his own garage, which is actually in the direction she'd have come. That might have been when she stopped."

"It's a pretty big problem," Travers said dubiously.

"There's a lot to come yet," Wharton told him. "Take that snoring business, for instance. She said she heard Philip snoring. Does that constitute an alibi? He always snored, didn't he? Very well then. She might just as well have said she heard the landing clock ticking."

Travers nodded but a trifle less dubiously.

"And another thing," Wharton went on. "What I'm telling you now, I got from the local police. It appears she has a gardener, an old boy of the name of Hughes. That Wednesday evening at knocking-off time she said to Hughes that Mr. Philip—Mr. Philip, mark you—wanted some plants that had been ordered from a local nursery, and it didn't matter about him coming to work at seven next morning—which was his time—but he was to go to the nursery and fetch the plants personally. Well, what about that?"

"On the face of it," said Travers, "it might be construed as a keeping of Hughes out of the way till someone had had time to look round by daylight and cover up anything suspicious that might have been left lying about by night."

"Exactly," said Wharton portentously. "I may add that the plants were the ordinary red and white daisies and Philip did actually plant them along the short drive to his garage. And just one other little thing. The lock of his garage had been filed. I saw it myself. Would a real honest-to-God car-thief have filed a lock like that?" He snorted. "He'd have hack-sawn it apart inside a minute. If that doesn't make that business look like a fake, then my name's not George Wharton."

Travers gave yet another shake of the head. "It's the old trouble, George. When we're looking for clues and pointers we seize on something that might have been perfectly normal in normal circumstances. What I can't get away from myself is roughly the same thing that strikes you—why anything at all should have happened at Severns on that night of all nights. Everybody in the house, I take it, sleeps normally for years, and then we get a night that was disturbed." He was giving his glasses a slow polish. "And, of course, we must take into consideration the fact that Severns, in these days of fast travelling and with a clear road at night, could be a matter of only fifteen minutes from here."

"Just my point," Wharton said, spreading his hands.

"I wonder," said Travers meditatively. "Could Henrietta possibly have had a hand in planting Sonia here for the honeymoon?"

"How do you mean?"

"Well, it'd depend on her relationships with Sir Raphael. Why shouldn't she have suggested to him that it would be only right and proper for his nephew Sidley to spend a day or two in what was after all the English home of the head of the family?"

Wharton nodded. "I'll tell you just what I learned from Sir Raphael's solicitors. Mind you, they knew they weren't talking to George Wharton, or I'd have been told damn little. One of the Powers That Be gave them a friendly tip before I got there, which was why I had a peep at the skeleton in the cupboard. For instance, there's a lot of truth in that rumor that the old boy's turned miser."

"Sidley more or less confirmed that," Travers said. "You remember how he spoke of his clothes."

"I also gathered that he suffers from harmless little delusions," Wharton went on. "He was knighted for handling that big Ertzenheim bequest for the Government, then he quarreled with everybody and moved himself and his collection over to France. I understand he's leaving everything to the French nation, so naturally they think very highly of him over there. They respect his privacy and his eccentricities."

"What precisely are the eccentricities?"

"Well, the fact that he's virtually a hermit. And he's miserly, as I said." His voice lowered. "In the strictest confidence I can tell you he was selling this place during the summer to cut down expenses. The solicitors had received instructions from France. Also he'd reduced Henrietta's allowance. When her husband died it was two thousand a year—which, I believe—was a flea-bite to him. Last year it had dropped to a thousand."

"Interesting, every bit of it," Travers said, "but it doesn't get us much forrader. By the way, did my name crop up in that interview of yours this morning?"

"Yes," Wharton said, "and I may as well tell you the truth. She mentioned your name and I was forced to remark that Mr. Travers was a well-meaning gentleman who—well, who occasionally exceeded his privileges." He chuckled speciously. "Just a little bluff on my part."

Travers was nodding away to himself. "Very subtle of you, George, and it may be even more so." He looked up. "What we want is information about Henrietta and everything to do with Severns. Why shouldn't I play myself off against you? Let me see her in the very near future and apologize for you."

He was smiling so delightfully that Wharton's glare faded.

"I get you. You worm yourself right into the affections, as they say."

"Exactly. Protect a helpless widow Against the bullying of people like yourself. Put her wise, so to speak."

"Helpless, my foot!" Then he remembered something of the morning's interview. "That cat business. I introduced the subject rather skillfully this morning and all the time I didn't quite know what I was getting at. Just tell me again what's the importance of it."

"There doesn't seem to be any—now," Travers said. "We were trying to connect Sonia up with some man. If she kept a cat and Philip Carne was looking after that cat for her—temporarily, of course, and in that old Bloomsbury flat of his—then there was a connection between her and him."

"I get you," Wharton said. "But from what Lewis reports, that's a dead end. It's Patrick who might have been the one in the lady's favour." He began gathering up his papers. "I'm going back to town in a minute or two. Conference on at half-past seven."

"See you on Monday then," Travers said. "No harm if I see the helpless widow in the meanwhile?"

"Why not?" said Wharton grimly. "What I shall be doing myself I can't say. It depends on what comes out of the pow-wow. There's more unlikely things than my dropping in on Sir Raphael."

Travers stared.

"Oh, yes," Wharton said. "Patrick Carne appears to be there, and the old boy is the only one in the family who hasn't been asked to throw any light on things. And his name keeps cropping up a bit too frequently for my liking."

"I think it's an admirable idea," Travers told him. "But if that place of his is the Hermit's Den plus Monte Cristo Cave affair one gathers it is, then you'll never be allowed to put your nose inside."

"Oh?" said Wharton. He made a grimace which might have been intended for a wink. "What about the majesty of the law? Still, I must be getting back to the Yard. We'll let you know anything that happens."

He accompanied Travers to the main door and waited till the Rolls was just about to move. Then Travers looked out.

"Any message for the widow?"

"Yes," said Wharton. "Tell her—" Then he broke off. Words failed him, and the only ones at the tip of his tongue would have startled the ears of the attendant Palmer.

But there were no flippancies in the mind of Ludovic Travers as he settled down to that forty mile drive, for what had dawned on him was that a wholly new factor had entered the situation, and that factor was Coales.

Admittedly the motive was slight, and yet, what did he and Wharton know? But the fact remained that if Sir Raphael was selling Montage Court, then Coales would leave what had been his home for best part of a lifetime, and what was for him a place of comfort and considerable pride. Yet how the killing of Sonia might affect the sale, Travers could by no means fathom; all he knew was that if that ghost yarn was an invention, or Coales's evidence was in any way unreliable, then the slow tentative building-up process begun by the law was no building at all, but only airy rubbish to be blown away by a puff of wind.

Then suddenly there came another idea, so novel and so urgent that instinctively he slowed down the car to let his thoughts have play. Coales, the old family retainer, who had known the Carne boys in their infancy and Henrietta since girlhood. Why should not his evidence have been not only biased but deliberately distorted? Suppose, for instance, he had actually seen Henrietta that night!

Travers was under no delusions about Henrietta. She might belong to a generation when women were at least not noted for initiative and cold-blooded remorselessness of purpose, but she was the exception who made her own rules. She was the kind to accept favors as homage, and she would take it as a matter of course that Coales should keep silence. Even that rheumatic leg of hers might have been part of the scheme, and at once his mind was busy with ingenious schemes to startle her at some unguarded moment and make her betray the fact.

And yet about everything there was always a doubt that was somehow stronger and more lasting than the fleeting intuitions. Nothing but vagueness everywhere, and no sooner did something appear which had an air of tangibility about it, than it too dissolved into doubt and uneasiness. Wharton was right. That was the one thing he was feeling in the very marrow of his own bones—that all the factors in the case had not been even cursorily examined and all the cards were very far from being on the table. Sir Raphael himself must be an essential, and the more Travers thought of him, the more he saw him as a central and looming figure. Wharton had been right, Sir Raphael's name had cropped up rather too much.

And once Wharton had seen him, the Breye circle would be at least complete, though how it would help, heaven alone might know. And the time factor was becoming urgent. Sonia might not have been dead more than a scant forty-eight hours, but already the alibi of the killer was becoming blurred, where one hour after the murder it might have stood out clear and sharp. Then the killer might have made some damning slip; now he was profiting by the delay to cover each slip and reinforce each link.

But when Travers drew near Pulvery the case began to be less of an oppression on his mind, and once he was inside the house it was altogether forgotten. There was a small dinner-party for Tom's birthday and at nine o'clock there was dancing. Travers was in charge of the gramophone till the time when dance music was on the air from the National.

Next morning a remarkably drowsy Travers awoke with something on his mind. In that split second the likely topics flashed—Henrietta Carne, Wharton and had he gone to France, Philip Carne and a cat in his arms, Patrick Carne—and then he knew. That problem of the wireless was what was worrying him. The thought had come the previous night, but even now it was far from clear, so as Palmer drew the blinds, Travers groped for the glasses and screwed up his eyes as he polished the heavy lenses.

Something arising out of what Wharton had said, how Patrick Carne had not turned off the wireless since that had been done for him automatically by the B.B.C. themselves. That was the key-word—*automatically*. Yet somehow the application had gone. That was the worst of those late nights, they fuddled the morning brains. For one quick moment he had seen some connection between turning off the wireless and turning it on, and now, puzzle his wits how he might, he could not recall what the connection had been.

But it would come back, he told himself as he dressed; and then with Tom at breakfast talking about golf, and then the golf itself and lunch at the clubhouse, it was not till tea that Travers once more found any leisure for thought. Even then what happened came rather as a flash of sudden revelation than as the answer to self-questioning and inevitable logic.

What happened was that tea was as usual in the small drawing-room, and that the eyes of Travers fell as by chance on the Sheffield tray with its tea-pot, milk-jug and sugar-bowl, and plated kettle on its stand with the heater beneath. It was the kettle at which he was all at once staring so intently.

"What's the matter?" Helen said, and had a look at the tray.

"Oh, nothing in particular."

"You don't put me off like that," she told him. "There *was-*something. You were staring and making the most hideous faces."

"Not hideous, surely!" He smiled. "Intent faces, perhaps." Then he frowned again. "Just the play of the light on the spout of that kettle. It had a rather curious effect."

At nine o'clock that evening he was called to the telephone It was Norris, ringing up from the Yard.

"Sorry to worry you at this time of night, sir, but the Super'll be back first thing in the morning."

"Back from where?"

"I thought he'd told you," Norris said. "He took the night plane to Paris on Friday after you'd seen him. He kept in touch with us, sir, and he was talking about coming back as soon as he heard the news."

"What news?"

"Sorry, sir. I forgot to tell you. They've found that plane at last, sir. Trove was there all right, but dead as mutton. That's all, sir, except that Vienna reports extraordinary developments."

"Good Lord!" said Travers. "What developments?"

"Don't know yet, sir. They haven't let us know. Well, that's all for the present, sir—"

"Wait a minute, Norris. You say Wharton's coming home in the morning. Could you make an appointment for him—and yourself too, if you like—at my flat at, say, three o'clock tomorrow?"

"I'll put it up to him, sir, as soon as I see him. Anything in the wind?"

"Quite possibly," Travers said. "I think perhaps I've busted Patrick Carne's alibi!"

XI
WHARTON INVESTIGATES

WHEN IN HIS earlier years George Wharton had satisfied himself that the man who could offer something extra would sooner or later get his chance, and when he had therefore followed a natural bent and specialized in French, he did himself a remarkably good turn. The chance came in the once notorious Simone Case, when his superiors were so impressed with the fact that he had repeated in the vernacular the long conversation between the brothers, that he was thereafter a marked man. And he had never allowed that French of his to grow too rusty; in fact it remained fluent, adequate enough in vocabulary and with an accent by no means insular. But that was all. He certainly could not think in it, and it is doubtful if he could have sworn in it with any degree of satisfaction or effect.

So he was glad to make that trip to St. Peranne, much as he hated flying. At Paris he was surprised to be met by an official of the Sûreté who gave him the Austrian message which had been telephoned from London during the first stage of the flight. An hour or so later Wharton took the night plane for Marseilles and arrived not much after dawn. A stroll along remembered haunts at the quays and he was ready for an early meal. There was never a breath of *mistral* and the day looked like being scorching hot, so that already he was unbuttoning his waistcoat as he made for a taxi rank to bargain for that twenty kilometer ride.

As he came out at the coast road his heart leapt at the familiar scenes; the trim villas set above the shore, the snug bays with water incredibly blue, the massed pines on the low bluffs and the red inland earth where men tended the young vines. So much had there been to recall that it was something of a shock when the auto stopped in the pleasant square of a little town and the driver announced that they were there.

Wharton's eyes ran seaward from a vantage point behind the church and at once spotted what could be no other than Sir Raphael's villa. Around it ran high hedges of mimosa and cypress, backed by tall matting against the *mistral*, and the house towered above more like some squat château than the anticipated villa of maybe some dozen rooms. The Villa Meyrac, it was called, according to Coales, who had also given information about Sir Raphael's English valet, Pettry by name, an old acquaintance of his own. Coales had spoken highly of Pettry; a devoted servant, he had said, and a man of standing in his profession.

It was nine o'clock then and as Wharton turned to make his way down to the sandy shore, he saw the gate of the villa open and a car emerge. It halted and a man appeared to be talking to some occupant of the car; then it moved on and the man bowed, backed through the heavy iron gate and closed it behind him. Wharton came back to the square again and waited. In a minute the car—a taxi undoubtedly—went by him in a cloud of dust and he caught sight of the passenger, and from Travers's descriptions, knew him for Patrick Carne.

So Carne was on his way to Marseilles and the return plane, which seemed reasonable and legitimate enough, with the only surprising thing the shortness of his stay. Five minutes later Wharton was on the beach before the villa, noting the lie of the land. The bay before it was closed, and ample for the alighting of a seaplane, while a landplane, he thought, could land along the line of beach itself. But the villa was now embowered in the trees that sheltered it from the east, and above the steps that ran to yet another entrance above the rocks, he caught a glimpse of lawns and flowers. All round, as he now saw, was a low wall surmounted by iron railings which the tall gates matched and of which they seemed to be a part.

He climbed the rocks to the west and came to the gate from which the taxi had emerged. It was closed but a bell-chain hung by the iron pillar. He tugged and waited and in a minute an indoor servant appeared. Wharton stated his business and handed over a card Without a single spoken word the man turned back to the house again and Wharton was left watching through the still-closed gate.

Five minutes this time, and another man appeared—the man who had ushered the taxi through the gate. He approached deferentially.

"You wish to see Sir Raphael, sir? I'm Pettry, sir, his confidential valet."

It was on the tip of Wharton's tongue to ask what the devil that might precisely be. Instead he returned Pettry's bow.

"Yes, on most important business."

"Sir Raphael wishes to be informed of the exact nature of the business, sir."

"Oh," said Wharton, and grunted. "Say it's to do with the death of his niece by marriage—Mrs. Sidley Cordovan, Miss Sonia Vorge that was."

Pettry gave him a look of puzzled inquiry. He was a short, plump man with a manner suave but remote.

"Sir Raphael has already been informed of the matter, sir. His nephew has just left, sir. Mr. Patrick Carne."

"I see," said Wharton bluntly. "And did Mr. Carne tell him who killed her?"

Pettry moved never a muscle. "Sir Raphael does not inform me, sir, of his private affairs. If you wait one moment, sir, I will see Sir Raphael."

"Any reason for me to stay behind these damn gates?" began Wharton, but the unhearing Pettry had already gone. It was another five minutes before he returned.

"Sir Raphael will see you at eleven-thirty, sir. He regrets the delay."

"Does he realize I've come all the way from England to see him?" Wharton said.

Pettry bowed. "I'm sorry, sir. I can only repeat Sir Raphael's instructions."

He bowed again and turned back to the house. Wharton was fuming. It was not the question of an affront or discourtesy to himself that roused his wrath, but that the law itself should be kept outside a locked gate as if it were some cheap tradesman whose credentials were being scrutinized. Sir Raphael, Wharton was indignantly assuring himself, might have been an international figure who had hobnobbed with princes and the Lord knows who, but the law of England, however modest its representative, was more important than Sir Raphael and his princes and his whole damn collection. The French might respect his eccentricities but he—George Wharton—would certainly have a thing or two to say when the time carne.

Rough heath country lay at the back of the gardens, and though there was no defined path, Wharton made his way along the tall hedge to circle the grounds and came out at a clump of pines that had caught hit eye The line of hedge turned east and then dipped. The *mistral* must have been violent of recent days for the mats were blown aside, and through the gaps he could clearly see the kitchen garden and the inner hedge that lay between that garden and the lawns. A few steps more and he was at the east wing of the house, with the hedge turning so near that the windows were a scant ten feet away. They were barred, he now saw, with long metal rods that ran from top to bottom, and then as he passed a new gap he saw all at once a turning on of lights within the house itself.

The eucalyptus trees threw him in deep shade, and as he stood there with a slit in the matting for a peep-hole, he was aware that some trick of lighting was revealing the interior of a whole room. It was a long room, its walls lined with pictures but devoid of all furniture. A man was standing with back towards him; an old white-haired man with stooping shoulders, and eyes raised apparently to one particular picture which he was studying, but what that picture was Wharton could not see, except that it was light in color and curiously sparkling.

A door must have opened and a man came in. He was carrying something long—a step-ladder, that was it. He seemed to be asking for orders. The old man must have indicated that one picture for the ladder was adjusted and the man—Pettry it was—mounted it. The old man steadied it with one hand and held the other out as if to grasp the picture when it was released. Then the old man left the ladder and seized the picture with both hands, and Pettry must have loosened the fastenings for the old man was carrying it away and out of Wharton's sight through what must have been an opened side door.

Wharton moved hurriedly on and in a couple of minutes was at the pine dump. There he sat with his back to a tree and his eyes on the sea beneath him, and as he filled his pipe and snuffed luxuriously at the scented air, his indignations were slowly leaving him, and he could think with even a kindliness of the old man of whom he had just caught so unconventional a glimpse. Every man to his own hobby, thought Wharton, and then the humorous side of something all at once was tickling his fancy, and he was chuckling to himself. Yes, he must certainly tell that to Mr. Travers.

But Wharton had a far different reception when he next came to that front gate and pulled the rope. Pettry appeared as if by magic, opened the gate and was ushering Wharton in with a bow.

"This way, sir. Sir Raphael will see you at once, sir. A remarkably fine morning, sir."

"One of the best," said Wharton. "And, by the way, Mr. Pettry, your old friend Coales sent his kindest regards to you."

"Indeed, sir?" His face had a smile that was all at once making it strangely human. Then it went and he halted just long enough to give a little bow.

"Thank you, sir. Perhaps you will do me the favor of returning the compliment, sir."

He was opening a door and Wharton stepped into a room that looked uncommonly like Pettry's own. Its window was unbarred and it looked out across the kitchen garden, where an old man was working with a spike-hoe among the clumps of artichoke.

"Sherry, sir? The cake is Sir Raphael's own special favorite, sir."

"What's that?" Wharton turned from the window to be aware of the table and the refreshments. "Ah! thank you, Mr. Pettry. I am a bit peckish."

"Perhaps you'll help yourself, sir. And pardon me, sir."

He was backing through a side door. It closed and Wharton peered that way, then turned to the cake. In five minutes the door was opening again and Wharton got to his feet as an old man came in. Pettry's voice was coming from the unseen rear.

"Mr. Wharton, Sir Raphael."

The eyes of the two men met. Sir Raphael was heavy-browed, shortish, and with something of the look of an Old Testament prophet. Wharton felt something suspicious, searching, and even malignant in those eyes of his, then the old man's head turned away and Pettry was placing a chair. He gave a kind of grunt, lowered his bulk into the chair, and Pettry took up his station behind it. A hand was waved and Wharton sat down too.

"You want to see me?"

It was monotonous, impersonal voice, somewhat guttural in tone, and the face had changed too, for the eyes now seemed dull and almost unseeing.

"Yes, Sir Raphael" He gave a little nervous clearing of his throat. The scene was far different from his imaginings and there was something Olympic and awesome about the old man himself. "I understand you are already aware of the death of your niece—Mrs. Sidley Cordovan."

"Yes," he said. "Sidley married her."

Wharton gave a quick look, "Of course, Sir Raphael. I understand your nephew, Mr. Patrick Carne, was here to tell you about it."

Pettry stooped suddenly and whispered. The old man listened, mouth partly agape and eyes dull as ever. Then he nodded.

"Patrick Carne came specially to tell me."

"So I understood, Sir Raphael. Now what we're wondering—Scotland Yard, that is—is whether you can throw any light at all on the matter."

He shook his head and his shaggy hair flopped as if the wind had caught it. "I know nothing—nothing at all."

"Well, we'd hoped you might," Wharton said. "But about the honeymoon, Sir Raphael I take it you know that she was spending the first few days of her honeymoon at Montage Court. Can you tell me how it was that Montage Court was chosen for that honeymoon?"

"She asked me herself. Sonia asked me."

Wharton beamed. "That was when you were last in London, Sir Raphael?"

"In London?" He was giving that same mouth-agape look.

"Yes, Sir Raphael. About a month ago,"

Pettry stooped again and whispered. The old man shook his head and it was Pettry who spoke.

"Sir Raphael's memory fails him sometimes, sir."

Wharton nodded sympathetically, and then was shaking his head. The gathering of information seemed hopeless, and already he was wondering if Pettry were not the man to nobble. So as a prelude to farewells he imparted a piece of news of his own.

"You might like to know, Sir Raphael, that the aeroplane has been found—the one poor Trove was killed in."

The dullness had gone from the old man's eyes. They were all at once alert and his chin was thrust out and he was staring.

"The plane? They've found the plane?"

"Well, yes," Wharton said, with a smile and a wave of the hands. "They always expected to find the plane, when the snows melted."

Then he was getting to his feet. Sir Raphael was hoisting himself from the chair, with Pettry helping him and somehow defending himself at the same time, for the old man was clawing at him and his voice was a bellow.

"Why wasn't I told? Why didn't he tell me?"

"There, there, there, sir! Please, Sir Raphael, please!" Pettry was soothing him but the old man was thrusting him off. He turned to Wharton, eyes glaring. "You've come to see my pictures!"

"Sir Raphael, I assure you—"

Pettry was making frantic signs for quiet as he began moving his master towards the door.

"That's all a mistake, Sir Raphael. Mr. Wharton didn't come to see the pictures, sir. He doesn't know a thing about pictures, Sir Raphael."

"Not a thing, sir, I assure you—"

The two were at the door, with Pettry making a backward sign for Wharton to remain where he was. The door closed behind them and in the corridor the soothing sounds still came to Wharton's ears. Then there was silence and he sank back in his chair again and began mopping his brow.

In two minutes Pettry was back, and he was his imperturbable self again.

"This way, sir," he said, and opened the door by which he and Wharton had entered.

"Just a minute," Wharton said, and held his ground.

"Not here, sir; I beg of you." Another bow and he was leading the way to the outer gate. Wharton went through, and, with a quick backward glance, Pettry followed him. Two yards left he stopped where the thick mimosa hid them from the house.

"Mr. Wharton, I ought to have warned you. Sir Raphael suffers from delusions, sir. They're harmless delusions, sir, but if I may say so, disconcerting to a stranger."

Wharton grunted. "What was the idea? Did he think I'd come here under false pretenses, to steal his pictures?"

"Something of the kind perhaps, sir." He shook his head. "The pictures are his very life, sir, if I may put it that way, and

he's been very upset these last few hours—about Miss Sonia . . .
Mrs. Cordovan, I should say, sir."

Wharton grunted again.

"That's why I think he was so upset when you mentioned
Mr. Trove's name, sir. He was very fond of Mr. Trove, sir—we
all were."

"Well, I'm much obliged to you," Wharton said. "But now
I'm here, though, I suppose you can't throw any light on the
murder?"

"Me, sir?" He shook his head. "England seems a long way
away nowadays, sir. When people come here, sir, it's the master
they come to see, not me."

"You were in England with him a month ago?"

"I accompany Sir Raphael everywhere," Pettry said, and not
without a touch of pride. "When I say everywhere, sir, I mean
on his walks or when he goes to the town. He rarely goes even to
Paris nowadays."

"What'd he go to London for?"

"I'm sorry, but I can't tell you, sir. He informed me he was
going, sir, and he went. We stayed one night at Miss Sonia's
flat—as she was then, sir—and returned the following day.
What happened, sir, I'm unable to say. I obtained permission,
sir, to see my only living relation, sir, a sister who lives at Sou-
thend." He bowed. "Now if you'll pardon me, sir, I must return
to the house."

Wharton moved off back to the town, and he was a satisfied
if in some ways a disappointed man. What he was now proposing was to take the early evening plane back to Paris, and in the
meanwhile have lunch and maybe make further inquiries. The
proprietor of the café-restaurant and the waiter both proved
garrulous enough but all he learned were reinforcings of the
things he had suspected before he left London and now knew
for himself. Sir Raphael was a very great man. Queer, perhaps,
but then who wasn't? Millions of francs that collection of his
was worth, but he never encouraged visitors, it was said, and at
night, of course, the grounds were patrolled.

There was gossip also about the servants and mention of a lady who had arrived in the bay more than once by seaplane, but Wharton talked and listened more like a man who is glad to get the rust off his French than one who cocks an ear for a hint let fall or waits for the vital word. Then when he had learned that Sir Raphael had been seen in the town on the vital afternoon, he relaxed indeed. The meal soothed him, the day was hot and old scenes and memories were all about him. By the time he was on his way to the aerodrome, he had no regrets.

Though that dominating figure of the old man, and the strangeness of that scene in the strange, colorless room was still the main background of his thoughts, it was the pleasure of a brief holiday that tuned his mood, and it was not till he called that night at the Sûreté and was waiting for Norris's voice over the phone, that he was George Wharton again, and thinking of work, England and east winds, conferences and inquiries and all the dreary round that comes under the heading of routine.

Norris's voice came. Wharton was grunting at the lack of news and firing the same old questions. Then he was all at once startled.

"There was one thing, sir. Mr. Travers is most anxious for us to go along to his flat at about three. He claims to have upset the alibi of that Patrick Carne."

"Upset it!" Wharton said. "How? Do you know?"

"I don't know a thing," Norris told him. "But you know what he's like, sir. If he says he's upset it, then we can take it it's upset."

Before noon next day Wharton was back in his room at the Yard, and the first thing Norris had to show him was the latest message from Vienna. It was a kind of liaison message from the Special Branch man who had been sent over on the first receipt of definite news.

Trove's remains identified but plane practically burnt out. Shot-mark back of skull. Both legs fractured. Site considerably nearer than imagined. Further developments imminent.

Wharton read it a second time, then merely looked at Norris with a raising of eyebrows.

"A bit complicated, sir, isn't it?" Norris said. "I mean if it was she who shot him and set fire to the plane?"

"It won't be our worry," Wharton said. "Not that I wouldn't like to know just what's meant by *developments*." He folded the copy carefully and put it in his pocket "I'd just as soon you didn't say anything to Mr. Travers about this when we see him this afternoon."

It was Norris's turn to raise eyebrows.

"No particular reason," Wharton told him airily. "But if he's going to get up to his conjuring tricks, I'd just as soon let him get his own rabbits out of the hat."

XII
CONCERNING AN ALIBI

LUDOVIC TRAVERS would sometimes speak of himself as the father of the flat, referring, of course, to a series of flats under one roof. Soon after the war he had inherited a semi-tenement block in St. Martin's, and with the idea of occupying one flat himself, had converted the building into a set of six, with, as the agents say, every conceivable modern convenience.

The time was an excellent one; not too late for spaciousness and genuine comfort, and far too early for the vulgarities. The rooms were large, a small restaurant saved bother about domestics and meals, the liftman acted as general factotum, and just across the road was a garage. Travers's own flat consisted of an emergency kitchen, Palmer's bed-sitting-room, a lounge-dining-room, work-room, two bedrooms and—again to quote the agents—all the usual offices.

Wharton and Norris arrived on time that Sunday afternoon, and Travers had returned from the country before lunch. There was some leg-pulling, Travers insisting that Wharton's trip to the South had given a definite sunburn. Wharton, taking a quick peep at himself in the mirror, seemed quite pleased.

"I thought the same thing when I was shaving," he said, and, as he took off his heavy coat: "Then you get back to this damn country and there's an east wind enough to cut you in half."

Travers drew the chair round the fire.

"Well, make yourself cozy, and you too, Norris. As soon as Palmer gets back, we'll have tea. And now tell us all about it."

Wharton waved aside the cigarettes and hauled out his pipe.

"Oh, no," he said. "Your turn first. What happened at Severns?"

"I'm afraid, nothing," Travers said. "As soon as I thought I'd tumbled to the fishy part of Patrick Carne's alibi, I was so busy that I didn't seem to have a moment Besides, I thought perhaps you'd like to concentrate on him first—that is, if you agreed with my findings."

Wharton grunted. "And what are the findings?"

"Sorry," Travers said, "but I can't tell you just yet. It all depends on Palmer, and he's out at the moment, as I just told you. When he comes in I think we might try an experiment or two."

Wharton grunted again, than cast an eye kitchenwards.

"I don't think I'd sit with my back to that open door if I were you. you're asking far a stiff neck."

Norris nipped up at once to close the door. Travers stopped him.

"Please don't, Norris. I don't feel a draught—really. Also I rather want to hear Palmer when he comes in." He smiled across at Wharton. "Now what about all these adventures of yours?"

Wharton, as a matter of fact, was by no means loath to begin. He had as yet said nothing, even to Norris, and two things were in his mind. In view of that evening's conference at the Yard, there was nothing like trying it out on the dog; moreover there might be comment and suggestion from his two listeners that might transform even the trivial into something important. Travers was the first to interrupt.

"Tell us some more about Sir Raphael. What's he look like nowadays, for instance?"

"It's hard to say," Wharton told him. "But I'd call him impressive. I mean, as soon as you clap eyes on him you know he's a somebody. Yet he didn't look anything, in a way. He was slovenly and untidy and"—he gave a sideways nod—"yet I don't know. I've run up against all sorts in my time, but he's one of what I'd call the big ones."

"An eminent Victorian," suggested Travers.

"Well, yes. He certainly looked much older than his age. I'd have put him at eighty instead of seventy-two or three."

"A fine house, was it?"

"Not my taste exactly," Wharton said. "Still, you can't have a miniature fortress and a home at the same time."

He went on with the morning's interview and described, not undramatically, the final scene when the old man had gone half-distracted from the room. Travers was shaking his head.

"So he is mad."

"Don't you believe it," Wharton said. "If I've given that impression, then I'll correct it at once. That fellow Pettry was right. The old boy suffers from delusions, otherwise he's quite sane. He simply lives for his pictures and the rest of the world isn't very clear. He's got a temper, mind you; I admit that You ought to have heard him bellow." He shook his head. "Half the time, though, he didn't appear to know what I was saying. But a kind-hearted old chap, I should say. That Sonia business was a nasty shock and it was my blurting out about Trove that set him off."

"And that's the lot?"

"Yes," Wharton said, and added a brief account of the subsequent talk with Pettry. Then he suddenly chuckled.

"I'll tell you something that struck me as rather funny. I wasn't in any particularly comic mood at the time, so I don't know quite why I did see the funny side."

He told them what he had seen through the window from the peep-hole in the torn matting.

"Lights on in the day-time," said the practical Norris. "That means he's got interior lighting same as they're fitting in the big museums nowadays so they can be opened to the public at night."

"I expect that's it," Wharton said, and went on to the moral of the tale. "So when I saw them taking down the pictures, what I thought to myself was: 'Some hell of a face you must have had. Some people count the silver before and after I walk in. You go one better. You put the valuables out of my reach!'"

He gave another valedictory chuckle, then was the official again.

"Well, quite a nice break in the proceedings, so to speak, and not altogether a waste of time. If I found out nothing else, I did find enough to take the old boy off our short list. Aeroplanes or no aeroplanes, he couldn't have been where he was and when he was, and at Montage Court the same night."

"And, with all apologies to Mr. Travers," Norris said, "it certainly looks as if Patrick Carne had nothing up his sleeve. He wasnt bolting or anything like it."

"Ah!" said Wharton roguishly. "That was a very bad claim on your part, Norris. You're delivering yourself into Mr. Travers's hands. He'd say, the stronger the alibi, the less need to bolt."

"Why not?" smiled Travers. "That seems to me perfectly good logic. What's the good of faking an alibi if you haven't any faith in it after all? Besides—"

Then, through that open kitchen door, came the sound of a clatter. It was as if something had been dropped, and on its heels came a secondary bang as of tin against tin. Wharton swivelled round in his chair and stared, but before he could speak, on came the wireless—a fruity, Anglican voice discussing, apparently, the sources of the Pentateuch. Wharton smiled.

"Palmer's back."

But Travers was putting on a look of enormous surprise.

"But he can't be!"

Wharton's eyes narrowed. "What do you mean?"

Travers pointed. Wharton and Norris looked round, and there was Palmer coming from the workroom, and Wharton knew well enough that the door through which he was coming was its only one.

"Wait a moment, Palmer, will you?" Travers said. "I ought to make it clear to you both that Palmer has been inside there ever since you arrived."

"Well, what's the idea?" Wharton challenged him.

"Patrick Carne's idea," Travers said. "You remember that Lidget—his neighbour—complained that when he came in at night, he was tight and knocked over things. Also he set the wireless going—and that's where you came in, George Lidget said Carne had at least the decency to switch off at midnight. You pointed out that he hadn't. The B.B.C. did that for him by closing down at midnight."

But Wharton was getting to his feet and making for the kitchen. The others followed, Travers still talking.

"Keep an open mind, George. I don't claim that what you see can't be improved on, but Palmer and I had the very devil of a time working it all out."

Wharton took one pace inside the kitchen and then halted. One quick look round and he was pursing his lips. Then his eyebrows lifted.

"What is this? A Heath Robinson imitation?"

"Now you're deliberately exaggerating," Travers said. "There aren't any elaborate contraptions. There's the power switch in the wall, exactly four feet above floor level. There's a piece of string on it, and the other end of the string is attached to the kettle. There are also two cake tins to assist the clatter."

Wharton smiled complacently. "And just how does the—er—model work?"

"Perfectly simply," Travers told him, and stepped inside the room to demonstrate. "Everything depends on the weight of a kettle when it's full compared with the weight when it's not. First you adjust the switch till it acts at the very slightest pull." He illustrated. "The height above floor level helps a lot. Then you fill the kettle and put it on the gas-ring or electric ring, and set the heat according to how long you wish it to be before the water all boils away. Meanwhile you've connected the switch and the handle of the kettle by string—wire would be better because there'd be no risk of burning—and to the middle of the string you tie two tins, and a weight. The lid's off the kettle and it's allowed to boil away. Then the time comes when the kettle weighs less than the tins and the weight, so the kettle is dragged over and falls. The tug pulls the wireless switch, and the tins and kettle make the clatter. The gas goes on burning harmlessly and that's all there is to it."

"*All* is right," said Wharton amusedly. Another complacent nod or two and he turned. "Do you honestly mean to tell us that"—he waved at the floor—"this sort of thing was what Patrick Carne hoped would save his neck? A man's neck depending on a contraption like this!"

Travers let out a deep breath.

"George, there are times when you can be really exasperating. I don't claim that this is the actual contraption, as you insist on calling it. What I claim is that when Lidget thought Patrick Carne was in his flat, he based those opinions on very unsubstantial grounds. If you took it for granted that Palmer was in the kitchen just now, aren't you rather in the same boat?"

Wharton shrugged his shoulders. "The two cases aren't parallel. My objection is—well, you won't be offended?"

Travers smiled. "I don't think it'll matter a damn to you if I am."

"That's unkind," Wharton said piously. "Still, I'll say it. How it strikes me is that it's just a bit—well, childish."

Travers smiled. "Naaman the Syrian; you remember, George? 'If the prophet had bid thee do some *great* thing, wouldest thou not have done it?'" Another smile. "If it's the loss of your tea that's disturbing you, take heart. I rather fancy it's now coming up from downstairs."

"You will have your little joke," Wharton said, and turned back to the lounge and the fire. "But suppose we do take all this business seriously. What chance is there of proving Patrick Carne used anything like the same methods to make that man Lidget think he was in the flat when he wasn't?"

"There's only one way," Travers said, "and I didn't like attempting it myself. Some charwoman or other must come in to keep the place in order. There's just the chance that she may have noticed something. One very strong point in our favor is that we should be able to quote the very morning when she might have seen something—which was the morning when she saw on the placards that Sonia Vorge was dead."

"Yes," Wharton said, and frowned. "But let's say the charwoman found water on the floor or a mark where the weight struck it, or a dent in a tin or the kettle. I say she wouldn't, because if he'd rigged up anything of the kind, then he'd have removed all traces as soon as he came in. Still, say he didn't. What help is it to us? I don't want to harp on that word *childish*, but what sort of a reception should we get if we tackled him point-blank? What would a jury think about it?"

"And another thing," Norris said. "He knows how the law stands as well as we do. He knows he needn't answer any questions. If he said anything, he'd say, 'All right, gentlemen. If I wasn't in my flat, it's up to you to prove exactly where I was.' And pretty fools we'd look trying to prove that."

"Ah, well," said Travers philosophically. "It's a wicked world and an exasperating one. Let's forget all about it and tackle the muffins. If they are muffins. I can never quite make out which are muffins and which are crumpets."

Wharton pushed back his plate, wiped his weeping-willow mustache with wide sweeps of his voluminous handkerchief, and then began fumbling for his pipe. Travers pushed the bell for Palmer to clear.

"The time's drawing along," Wharton said. "Six o'clock for that conference, wasn't it, Norris? You're coming, I hope, Mr. Travers?"

"Heaven forbid," said Travers. "All I ask is to be let get on with some job."

Wharton took his old seat "Well, I'll tell you what I shall suggest. Sir Raphael Breye we can disregard, and Philip Carne. But about Patrick, I'm a bit dubious."

"May I mention something that occurred to me just now?" Travers said. "I'll put it in the form of my hypothesis of the happenings of that particular night. Patrick Carne laid the alibi train ready and left his club—or even his flat again—at, say, half-past ten. I don't know what means he employed, but he could have been at Montage Court in half an hour, considering how clear the roads were. But he reached his flat again at about one o'clock, and he entered by his side-door, and very suspiciously. So suspiciously, in fact, that a constable—as you remember—took him for a burglar and after a minute or two, knocked him up. Patrick shot on a dressing gown, ruffled his hair, took off his socks and put on slippers, and then, all sleepy, spoke to the constable and even conducted him over the flat. My point is that we thus ought to be pretty well sure in our minds that wherever Patrick Carne went, he went somewhere, and he came home from that somewhere at about one o'clock."

Wharton turned to Norris. "We'll keep him under observation from now on. With regard to my dear friend Henrietta, I take it you're adhering to your scheme about her, Mr. Travers. You'll worm yourself clean into her confidence, so to speak, under the guise of protecting her against the hardhearted police. Who's left now?"

"Coales," Travers said, and proceeded forthwith to state a case.

"There may be something in it," Wharton said. "He may look one of the righteous ones, but so did Charlie Peace." He nodded. "I'll tackle Coales myself. He needn't have done the actual killing but that's no reason why he shouldn't be shielding the one who did. He may be hand in glove for all we know."

"And Sidley Cordovan?" Travers suggested tentatively.

"Wait a minute," Wharton said, and began looking through a collection of papers from his breast pocket. "I had a fair amount of time for thinking on that journey and I devoted quite a lot of time to Mr. Cordovan." He adjusted his antiquated spectacles and then peered as usual over their tops. "Make any case you like against him. Say he faked whatever you like, but answer me one question. No hedging, but a yes or no. This is the question. When he and his wife came up that night to that lounge room, did he dream for a moment that—well, in blunt terms, she was not going to sleep with him?"

He leaned back, lips pursed, and waited.

"I say he certainly expected her to," said Norris.

"I agree," said Travers, "with the proviso that he wasn't any too happy."

"Right then," said Wharton triumphantly. "Then it couldn't have been he who brought the dope. Your answers make him the victim, not the attacker. And one other little thing. If he planned murder, where does the rope come in?"

"Yes," said Norris meditatively. "The hanging rope."

Travers shook his head. "I don't know that we've given enough time to that rope."

"There'll be time," said Wharton confidently. "We're getting on, even if it's slow." He got to his feet and knocked out his pipe in the grate. "Three suspects to concentrate on and one for each of us. That's what I'm recommending." His hand went out to Travers, then it drew back, and an expression of dismay came over his face.

"Why didn't you remind me, Norris? Here we are, going away, and I might have forgotten to tell Mr. Travers that latest news from Austria!"

But he took care not to catch Norris's eye as he found the paper and handed it to Travers. Travers read and was too astonished for immediate words.

"Makes you think, does it?" said Wharton.

"Think?" said Travers. "Why, it's an earthquake!" He shook his head. "What do you make of it, George?"

"Not much—just at present," Wharton said, and gave an ironical smile. "Norris and I rather expected you'd have some theory or other."

"Theory," said Travers. "It's the sheer hard sense of it that worries me. *Shot in the back of the head*. That can only mean she shot him."

"Not necessarily," Wharton said.

"Then he committed suicide while the plane was alight," Travers told him. Then he hooked off his glasses and began polishing them. "*Site nearer than imagined*—doesn't that make things clear?"

"Well, what happened?"

"I don't know," Travers said. "But recalling various things, I think this is not far out. The time of the departure of the plane from Russia was not advertised, as no doubt you know, therefore there wasn't any public anxiety about the plane's being overdue at Paris, or wherever it was bound for. Well, it crashed, or made what looks like a forced landing. That poor devil Trove had his legs smashed and Sonia escaped with little more than a shaking. She knew they couldn't get help unless by a miracle, so she took what food there was, and knowing he hadn't a chance, shot him and set fire to the plane to conceal the fact. When she luckily stumbled across that forester she made out that she'd been wandering for two days, whereas she might have been only an hour or two."

"It couldn't have been too near," Norris pointed out, "or the burning plane would have been seen."

"That country is all mountains and valleys," Travers said. "On one side of a ridge you'd never suspect what was happening on the other. Then of course snow was falling and that buried the remains. And as she gave a wrong idea of its whereabout, what little searching they did was in altogether the wrong district."

"It's a pretty horrible business," admitted Wharton. "As far as we and this case are concerned, it certainly proves a few things. That woman had no more heart than this spectacle case of mine. She was a hellion, out and out."

"Yes," said Travers. "And I'd give a goodish bit to know just what those *developments* are."

"All in good time," Wharton said blithely. Then out went his hand. "Well, thank you for what I'd call a real first-class tea; and thank you, Palmer, for looking after us. And that experiment you and Mr. Travers took all that trouble over. Most interesting and ingenious. It mayn't be a lot of help but it just shows."

But what precisely it showed he left in the air. At the corridor door he shook hands with Travers yet again.

"Well, thank you once more. Anything that turns up you'll be told of at once. Some time tomorrow, Henrietta—isn't that it?"

"That's it," said Travers gravely.

He watched the two enter the lift and he was still smiling to himself as he came back to the room. A specious old humbug, Wharton, but one of the best. But there was something he was keeping to himself, Travers was sure enough of that, and at once stretched out his long legs to the fire again and with fingertips together, began puzzling his wits as to what it was.

Meanwhile the lift took Wharton and Norris to the entrance hall. Wharton passed through the swing doors with never a word, but once on the outside pavement he halted. His voice was low and confidential.

"What'd you think of that busted alibi?"

Norris gave him a look, wondering which way the cat was expected to jump. Then he spoke his real mind.

"I thought it was damn clever. I believe that's what Carne actually did, or near it."

"So did I," said Wharton. "Looks as if we've got a line on the man we're looking for." He gave a sideways nod. "Shouldn't be surprised if this case is over inside the week."

XIII
MORNING FOG

BEFORE BREAKFAST Travers rang up the Yard and succeeded in getting hold of Norris.

"I'm going down to Severns in an hour or so," he said, "and I'd like you to do something for me. It's to do with Mrs. Carne. If I make her mind uneasy and she decides to go to Montage Court, will you have someone there to verify the visit?"

Norris said that could be managed but he doubted if there could be any listening in.

"Anything about those Austrian developments?" Travers asked.

"Nothing yet," Norris said. "But we've got a line on Stavangel. His mother was a Vorge, sister of Sonia's father. I'm talking about the real Stavangel of course, sir."

Travers said he understood, and was ringing off when Norris added a further piece of information. Menzies had been at that evening conference at the Yard and he and an additional expert were positive that the knife had been pressed home rather than suddenly and violently thrust. The edges of the wound and the course of the knife had both shown it.

"And what did you people deduce?" Travers asked him.

"Between you and me, sir," Norris said, "it landed us all properly in the soup. Remember when we first saw that bed, sir, and how we considered someone else had been in it besides her? And what was said about someone stooping over her and kissing her and then pushing the knife in?"

"I remember," Travers said. "I think we'd lost sight of it recently, but I remember."

"Well, there we are, sir," concluded Norris. "If that doesn't make you start to think of Cordovan again, then you're different from what I am."

It was almost ten o'clock when Travers was approaching Severns and the idea came to him to take the other fork of the lane and come to the house by the garage way. So he slowed down as he neared the short drive and what should he see but the doors of Philip's garage wide open, but no car there.

So Travers left his own car on the verge, and then became aware that a man was working in the long shrubbery that lay behind the garage and extended round towards the road, as a kind of shield for the gardens and house. The shrubbery was thin and the man appeared to be pushing a light roller among the shrubs and trees. When he caught sight of Travers he left his rolling and came towards the garage and there the two met.

"Good morning," said Travers. "Are you Mrs. Carne's gardener?"

"That's me, sir. Hughes, sir."

"I was passing," Travers said, "and I saw Mr. Philip Carne's garage open so I wondered if he'd been down. As a matter of fact I rather wanted to see him."

"He's coming tomorrow, I believe, sir," Hughes said. "I had the garage open to give it a good clear out. And to get that old roller of mine out."

"It looks clean enough to me," smiled Travers.

"So it ought, sir, considering I've just cleaned it. Them rabbits it was as made all the mess."

He was pointing to a hutch that now stood by a decrepit kind of potting shed in the further shrubbery.

"The missus would have them in the garage in the winter and what with tools and one thing and another, it was a proper mess. Her rabbits, they was. If they'd have been Mr. Philip's, he'd have had them out long ago."

Travers had a sudden idea. "I used to keep rabbits when I was a boy. What sort were these?"

"What we used to call Belgian hares," Hughes said. "Rare fine coats, they had; I'll say that for them. I reckon that's why they was took."

"You mean, stolen?"

"That was about it," Hughes said. "Went clean as a whistle and nothing ever found out. A fortnight ago that was. Them old gypsies, I reckon. Now Mr. Philip have told me to clean out the hutch and put it somewheres else. I told him I had cleaned it out after the rabbits went, but no, that wouldn't satisfy him. I had to clean it out again. Least, I shall do when I get time."

Travers was gathering that Hughes was an old family servant and with a will of his own.

"And what are you doing with the roller?" he asked.

"Well, sir, all this part behind the garage we've put down to grass. I sowed the seed about an hour ago and raked them in and now I'm rolling."

Travers nodded. "And what's the precise idea?"

"Well, sir, you may ask that question and get all sorts of answers," Hughes said. "I will say this for it though, We ain't having grass over there where the shrubbery is thick, but we're having it here where it's thin. Mr. Philip reckons that while I'm hoeing up weeds, which I am doing as soon as there's the least drop of rain, then I might as well be pushing the lawn-mower. The grass'll look better too."

"I don't know that it won't," Travers said "It seems to me you're going to be remarkably smart, what with these daisies and things."

"Daisies," said Hughes, and grunted. "They look smart enough, sir as you say, but there's them as have to weed 'em and keep 'em clean."

Travers smiled. "Yes, it's a trying world. Mrs. Carne at home, by the way?"

"I believe she's gone to Sevenoaks, sir. Let me see now. Yes, sir, she have gone. Monday morning she always go and change her books."

"I think I'll wait till she gets back," Travers said, and proceeded to move the Rolls on through the main gate. Henrietta's garage was open and as he rang the bell he hoped it would not be the deaf maid with whom he might have to talk. But with the cat away, the mice were playing, for he heard a laughing and talking somewhere in the house, and the youngish woman who opened the door was still smiling about something.

"Mrs. Carne in?"

"No, sir." Her face was prim at once. "We're expecting her back at any minute though."

"Then I think I'll wait," Travers said, and was once more shown into the drawing-room. The maid seemed the jolly kind who would not regard smalltalk with suspicion, though just what he could ask her he hardly knew.

"Does Mr. Philip Carne happen to be in?"

"Oh, no, sir. He hasn't been down for a day or two, sir."

"Curious," said Travers, and frowned. "I had the idea he was here. I'm sure he told me he was working. He always works when he's down here, doesn't he?"

"Oh, yes, sir. He works in his room upstairs."

"His bedroom?"

"Yes, sir. It's a work-room too, sir." She smiled as she told him that. Travers smiled too.

"Difficulties, are there?"

She gathered his meaning. "It doesn't do for anyone to g
in there, sir. Even madame wouldn't go in." She cocked an ea
and shot a look through the window, "Here madame is now, sir
Would you tell me your name, sir, please?"

"My dear Mrs. Carne." Travers bent gallantly over the out
stretched hand. "So sorry to call at such awkward times."

"My dear boy!" Perhaps Henrietta had definitely placed
Travers in that rather vague past which was her own Golden
Age, for she seemed whole-heartedly glad to see him. When he
had moved the settee nearer the fire he placed her stick at her el
bow and drew his own chair in. Then there was some talk about
the sketch, and how well it looked now it was varnished and
framed. Henrietta looked tragically round at the flamboyancies
that adorned the walls.

"You will understand, Ludovic, how I feel sometimes. When
I'm alone in this room sometimes I can feel myself surrounded
with ghosts."

Travers forebore a smile, his sympathies being with the
ghosts. Then he was aware that the remark had given him an
opening.

"That reminds me." His voice sank impressively. "I must tell
you why I thought I'd better call. You had a visit, didn't you
from a Superintendent Wharton of Scotland Yard?"

"Wharton?" she said. "Oh, yes. of course. A rather bizarre
individual, and most talkative."

"I'm afraid he bothered you somewhat," Travers said, "so
came to explain—and help. If he should by any chance worry
you again—"

"Worry?" There was a world of ironical amusement in the
word. "My dear boy! the man's a mountebank."

Travers smiled dryly. "You and I have to take the world as it
is, unfortunately, and not as we'd prefer it. He may be a mounte
bank but he's a highly important person. Unless you have some
one like—well, like myself, to act as a kind of buffer, he can make
himself very unpleasant, and be well within his rights."

He had spoken with such obvious sincerity that she looked mildly disturbed.

"But I don't understand."

"Let me explain," he said gravely. "You knew my uncle was Chief Commissioner." He hurried skillfully past that. "I therefore often become aware of things which are confidential and important. It's desirous, you will admit, that every criminal should be caught and suitably punished, but what you are concerned in is something more than ordinary crime. Murder—that's what brought Wharton here."

She drew herself frigidly up. "Are you suggesting that this man Wharton presumed to think I was in any way concerned with this murder?"

Travers refused to smile. "Mrs. Carne, I know I can trust you, but that's not enough. Before I tell you something that's even more than confidential, you must promise me never to speak a word to a living soul."

"But you're being mysterious."

He sighed. "Ah, well. I suppose I must tell you, promise or not." He glanced round and his voice sank to a whisper. "This is what the police know, and why Wharton came here. The one who murdered Sonia was actually seen just after the murder!"

"My dear Ludovic!" Her eyes were bulging.

"Wait a minute," he said, and gave another glance round. "Coales saw the murderer and the murderer saw Coales, so the murderer pretended to be the Montage ghost, and nearly scared Coales out of his wits. Now do you see the way in which you yourself may be concerned?"

It was noteworthy, he thought, that she should even trouble to think. She frowned; a quick, apprehensive look flashed across her face, then went.

"I'm sorry to be so obtuse, but I still can't see."

"Who knew about the Montage ghost but the members of the family?"

"Who knew?" She smiled. "Hundreds of people, my dear Ludovic. All those who read my poor dear sister's experience. Generations of servants."

Travers shook his head. "I may tell you that in conjunction with other information in their possession, the police—Superintendent Wharton, if you like—are convinced that the pretended ghost could have been only a member of the family. Mind you," he told her hastily, "I don't in any way identify myself with that view. How could I? It virtually says—well, something too preposterous for words. You and I know only too well who the members of the family are."

"As you say—preposterous." But she was frowning again.

"And now something about which I must have your solemn promise," Travers said. Then all at once he was making for the door, opening it and looking along the corridor. A mysterious nod and he was taking his seat again.

"Suppose Coales actually recognized the murderer! Suppose he's refusing to speak, out of a mistaken sense of loyalty to the family! Suppose it's only a question of time before the police make him open his mouth!"

She was staring, and for the life of him he could not have told if it were from incredulity or alarm. Then the thin blue lips went tightly together.

"I'm sorry, but I must refuse to credit any such thing."

Travers raised hands despairingly to heaven.

"Well—there we are. I've done my best and taken chances, and I can't do more. Sidley's not concerned, I must tell you that straightaway. Therefore if the remainder of the family—shall I be blunt?—if you yourself and Philip and Patrick, have to have your movements and private affairs inquired into by people like Wharton, then you mustn't blame me."

He smiled then as he got to his feet.

"Still, perhaps I'm being too much of an alarmist. If I've done nothing else I've put you on your guard."

"You're not going already?"

"Afraid I must," he said. "I'm hoping to keep Wharton and the police at a distance for you but if they should happen to turn up, I wouldn't like them to know I've been here. By the way, I thought you were looking amazingly well."

She ignored the remark altogether, and as he shot a look at her he noted the quick shake of the head.

"You've disturbed me very much, Ludovic."

"No, no," he said quickly. "Please don't allow yourself to be disturbed."

"I've read things," she said. "It's possible for a perfectly in-nocent person—" She broke off there and with a smile that was more like herself, reached for her stick. "I'm grateful to you, Ludovic, but I think I can deal with any impertinences myself."

"Philip's not likely to be down soon?"

"Some time this week," she said. "He's had the telephone put in, you know."

"Thank you," he said, and took the hint. "You're unable to re-peat what we've been discussing so I might do worse than warn him too. Patrick also."

His hand went out to help her from the settee.

"Curious," he said, "how your two boys should be so differ-ent. Both so clever in such different ways."

"But very fond of each other," she said quickly. "At least, I should hardly have said that. Philip, as the elder brother, was always devoted to Patrick, you know. But different, as you say. Philip is very high-strung, you know. His work, and the people he associates with, poor dear." She gave a little shudder. "Pat-rick was always detached; less easy to read."

"Children must be very fascinating," he said. Then all at once he was staring. "Good Lord!"

Her eyes followed his.

"A mouse!" he said. "I'm positive I saw a mouse!"

Henrietta moved never a muscle except to click her tongue annoyedly.

"I must really do something about those maids of mine. It's my belief they encourage the creatures in. I see it's raining. I do hope you haven't left your windows open."

"I expect they'll be all right," Travers told her. "Please don't come any further. It's quite impossible outside." Once more he stooped over the hand and the arched wrist. "So nice to have seen you again. Anything I can do, let me know."

* * *

It was an introspective and sheepish Travers who drove towards Sevenoaks in the lashing rain. But he was not taking the main road. That morning he had looked up a route that avoided Sevenoaks and yet made the journey to Montage no more than a mile longer, and now he was proposing to test it for speed, bearing in mind that at night it would be void of traffic.

As for his thoughts, he kept them from the main happenings of the morning, though now and again he would wince when they came inadvertently back to him. The rain, he said, would be good for those grass-seeds which Hughes had just sown, though the scheme seemed a cock-eyed one and the kind of thing to be evolved by an unpractical and fancy mind like Philip Carne's. Far better to have grubbed out shrubs and trees and then have grassed the plot than to have left all sorts of obstacles in the way of the lawn-mower. Besides, however closely a gardener worked there would always be long untidy grass around the stems of the shrubs and trees themselves.

But it was curious about Henrietta keeping Belgian hares. Some sentimental link with the past, perhaps, and pets that had been kept when she was a girl.

I had a dove and the poor dove died

The line came to him, and though it sounded somehow wrong, it set him to wondering about the stealing of the hares. Curious again that gypsies should have broken into the garage, or was it that someone had nipped in while Hughes had the garage open?

Or—more intriguing thought—was Philip himself the thief? Had he taken the hares—or hare—to that Bloomsbury flat and kept it there? But no. That hardly tallied with the account given by the hole-and-corner man who said he had seen Philip airing a pet some days before the apparent loss of his mother's hares. Or had he one hare in town, and his mother two at Severns? And if so, why?

The whole thing was so fantastic that Travers gave it up, only for his thoughts to go back to the ridiculous exhibition he had given throughout that morning. He had blethered and postured and been mysterious, and maybe all the time she had been keeping the ironic laughter to herself. But that was hardly right. Henrietta might not have been in the least degree scared, but she had done some furious thinking, and to have made her frown and lose her poise was something of an achievement.

As for that mouse experiment, when he had fondly hoped she would discard her stick and mount a chair or flee, that had been more than a fiasco, and somehow he felt a dim ironic gratitude that she had treated the outbreak with just the contempt it deserved. Then something else struck him—whether or not one could arrive at a parent from her children. Could the truth about Henrietta be arrived at by making her a compound of Philip and Patrick?

Then the sight of Montage Court cut short ideas and introspections. The road he had taken was even quicker than the one through the town, and unless one had particularly bad luck, never a constable would have been met. So Travers shot his own car on past the Court and made for the arterial road. As he drove now he was more resigned. The morning—as an inquiry—had been wasted, but as pure morning it had had its points. One might, for instance, do worse than insinuate a Henrietta, if cleverly enough camouflaged, into a book. Which reminded him. After lunch he would try to get hold of Philip Carne. And what exactly would be the pretext? The same as the morning's, or something new? Travers, in any case, was once more at the old game of working things out, and all the time the rain was lashing down.

He was late for lunch and it was two o'clock when he drew a chair up to his own fire. Then the telephone bell went—Norris ringing up from Montage Court.

"Thought I'd let you know, sir, that was a pretty lucky guess of yours. They were along at half-past eleven."

"They?" said Travers. "Who're they?"

"Well, the one you know, sir. Mrs. C . . ."

"Hear anything?"

"Never a thing, sir. I was in the bedroom, sir—you know, where I'm the only one's got a key. I took a peep out and she was in the gallery with Coales. Reckon he was showing her round."

"Nothing else?"

"No, sir. Nothing else at the moment."

"Thanks very much then," said Travers; and, just before he hung up: "You might like to know, by the way, that the lady in question has been keeping Belgian hares!"

XIV
AFTERNOON SUN

TRAVERS SETTLED into his chair again, long legs stretched towards the fire and fingertips together. The windows were still wet with rain but a furtive sun was peeping through and he could see blue sky with clouds that raced wildly. But the east wind was still keen so that the thought of it made the fire more cozy and there was a pleasure in the prospect of a spell of concentrated thinking.

The thoughts at first were scattered but soon they gathered themselves about Sir Raphael Breye, that central figure who, even when unseen, had appeared to be the bourne to which all suspects returned. Wharton had been much impressed by him, and a man who could impress Wharton was impressive indeed. Eccentricities and even delusions there might be, but apparently the mere shell of the man had shown something great.

Yet, thought Travers, greatness and courtesy should somehow go hand in hand, and it was strange that a man of Wharton's own importance should have been kept waiting outside a locked gate and have had his interview so coolly deferred. No other proof was needed of the mental deterioration of Sir Raphael, for in his prime he would have been well aware of the significance of a call from one of the senior officials of Scotland Yard.

As for Wharton's little joke about taking down the pictures, that had rather misfired. A man enamored of his own collection would always be experimenting. Then Travers suddenly

frowned. Would not a collector rejoice at the prospect of showing somebody over that collection, whether that somebody were
an expert or not? Curious too how Wharton had been shown,
not into Sir Raphael's own room or study but into a room bare
of pictures; the room apparently belonging to Pettry, the confidential valet. And why should Sir Raphael have had that queer
outburst of temper and accused Wharton of coming speciously
to get a view of the pictures?

One reason only, thought Travers. Sir Raphael had become
a miser of even his own pictures and grudged others a sight of
them, and in any case there was no point in building up theories
based on the remarks and outbursts of a man not wholly bal-
anced in mind. So the thoughts of Travers shifted to Henrietta
Carne, and how she revolved about the impressive figure of her
brother. She, of course, was wholly dependent on him, except
for what she might have saved out of his bounty. At his death
too, she and her sons would doubtless be the major heirs, with
Sidley Cordovan of course. That collection of pictures might be
going to the French nation but there would be quite a good sum
to be shared.

Then there was Patrick, the younger of Henrietta's sons; Patrick, the dark horse, about whom everything was colorless and
highly proper, and he too had been in contact with Sir Raphael.
When the old man had come to England—or would it be more
correct to say, had been escorted by Pettry to England?—Patrick had been one of the select two who had seen him. It had
been Patrick who had conveyed to his uncle the news of Sonia's
death, and everything about that visit had been what one should
have expected from Patrick Carne—smoothness, discretion, and
a tremendous propriety.

Then Travers's thoughts took a quick detour. Maybe Patrick
Carne—though he never advertised the fact—was in receipt of a
private income from his uncle. Colonel Faujoie had never rung
up about that confidential inquiry. Perhaps it was harder than
he had imagined to discover with any accuracy just how much
Patrick depended on bridge for a living. Curious too, thought
Travers, how that very evenness of everything about Patrick

Carne made one take him for much older than he was. He was still a young man, only thirty-six or seven, and in the prime of life. Not so strange after all, perhaps, that he had been able to leap like a cat out of the way of that taxi.

As for Sonia, she seemed always to have had contacts with Sir Raphael. What lay behind that last visit of his to her flat? Did she know only too well the state of his mind, and did she therefore arrange with Pettry to bring him to where he would not be disturbed or pestered? Hardly like Sonia to take thought for others, unless Sidley Cordovan's suspicions were true—that Sonia and Patrick were trying to influence the old man in the matter of his will.

Then there was Maurice Trove, who also had been a favorite. A horrible business, that forced landing, and Travers winced at the thought of the smashed limbs and Trove with nothing but Sonia between him and a dreadful death. It was like her to have seen no other way out but the ruthless one. A swift decision and a swift shot—and yet, why fire the plane? Why not have shot Trove in the temple and have left the gun as evidence of suicide? Did Sonia shoot first and panic later? Hardly like her to make mistakes or panic. That brain of hers had been too cold and deadly in its calculating. And, above all, why pretend that the landing had taken place miles from where it did? Was she distraught and had she wandered for hours in circles? Again, hardly like Sonia.

Then the telephone bell rang. Travers, rising from his chair, was not aware that the sound marked the end of speculation and uncertainty, and that within the space of minutes the sure glimmerings of truth would suddenly be seen.

"Ah! it's you, Mr. Travers,' Wharton began. "There's some news at last. It doesn't help us a great deal but it's interesting. It appears the Austrian authorities had been making an exhaustive examination of that burnt-out plane, and they discovered something almost at once. I don't quite know the technical terms but the plane was streamlined and had a specially shaped fusillage. You following me all right? . . . Well, on each side there were slots and one of these was a kind of secret space—a long, thin space—and, here's the important thing, they found a mass of charcoal stuff inside it as if something had been kept in it. That's what they've kept us hanging about for—to find out just what it was. Now a Herr Professor with a name I can't pronounce, but he's in the Ministry of Fine Arts, pronounces the mass authoritatively as having been two oil paintings. From a subsequent analysis of pigments he hopes to determine their age, so the message says. Now what do you think of it?"

"You tell me what you think of it," Travers said.

Wharton grunted. "All right. I'll do the telling, and I doubt if you'll pick any holes in it. The Bolshies have been disposing secretly of their best pictures and Trove and the Vorge woman had the job of smuggling them out of the country. Sir Raphael was buying them, which was why first of all he had grown so miserly—you know, raising the cash to pay for them—and secondly why he didn't want me or anybody else to clap eyes on them. They were for his own private delectation, so to speak."

"But why all that roundabout aeroplane method of delivery, and in midwinter?"

Wharton chuckled. "I guessed you'd ask that. But listen to this—the real theory this time. It wasn't the Russian Government that was selling but some Trotskyite or official who saw his way clear to a nice little bit of private graft. He got into touch with Sir Raphael, and it was all fixed up. Officially that plane trip was no more than a minor long-distance flight but the pictures were smuggled aboard for the return trip. Well, what about it?"

"Sounds all right to me," Travers said.

Wharton chuckled again. "I thought it would. It explains why Pettry and the old boy started taking the pictures down—I'll wager they've had a load or two before. It also explains the old boy's trip to London; arranging with Sonia for another flight."

"Yes," Travers said. "And you realize, of course, that it makes Sonia out to be a pretty cold-blooded murderess. The plane was fired not so much to conceal the shooting of Trove as to destroy evidence of the pictures and not incriminate the seller—or the buyer, if it comes to that."

"Oh, yes," Wharton said. "It all dovetails in. I had a fairly unprofitable quarter of an hour with our friend Coales, by the way. I couldn't find a flaw in his evidence anywhere. How'd you get on with the widow?"

"About as unprofitably," Travers said. "The usual thing: no end of things that might stand out and then have nothing to do with the case. You knew she was along to see Coales?"

"I've jotted it down," Wharton said. "Why did she go? Sheer curiosity, after what you'd let fall?"

"I shouldn't be surprised," Travers said. "In spite of an implied promise of strict confidence, I wouldn't trust her an inch."

Travers resumed his seat before the fire and he was aware that the last part of his talk with Wharton had been words that had done little more than drum in his ears. Something urgent was beating on his brain and as he hooked off his glasses and blinked away at the light that now streamed through the windows, he gave a sudden start. He had it!—not the whole truth perhaps, but something of the core of which the murder of Sonia had been only an off-shoot.

March the twentieth, when Rowlandson's had been playing in some bridge competition or other, and Lord Wryde had been a member, with Patrick Carne, of the team that had represented their club. And Patrick Carne would be playing again that same evening—and maybe the afternoon too.

In a flash Travers was at the phone and ringing up Rowlandson's, and he made no bones about giving his own name.

"Are you people playing the Chippendale in some competition or other?"

In the evening, he was told. The Smythe-Parkinson Cup was only a minor affair and the session would probably be from eight o'clock to eleven-thirty, with a return encounter at the Chippendale the following week.

"Mind telling me your team?" Travers asked.

"Oh, no," he was told. "It's the Hon. Stuart McGaine, P. Carne, Colonel Faujoie and H. J. Laurimere."

"Just what I wanted to know," Travers said. "It's Colonel Faujoie I'm after. He doesn't happen to be in the Club at the moment? If he is you might get him to the phone for me, will you?"

In five minutes Faujoie was speaking.

"Hallo, Travers. I know just what you want me for, but it didn't slip my mind. I haven't been able to get all the evidence. It was rather more intricate than I thought."

"Don't worry about that," Travers said. "Something far more urgent has turned up. Are you in the mind for a job of work—Bulldog Drummond stuff? The hell of a row if we're found out and quite a lot of excitement if we aren't?"

"Lead me to it," the Colonel said.

"Right," said Travers, and glanced at the clock. "Hop a taxi at once and you'll get here in time for tea."

Travers was pleased about Faujoie, the man who seemed built for the job. He was a widower, for one thing, and his house at Hadley Wood lay near enough to the end of the Cockfosters Tube. A fine place too, and a perfect setting. And the Colonel a man to keep his mouth shut when necessary and to open it to some purpose when occasion required.

Travers had concluded some more telephoning, and the tea was on the table when Faujoie arrived. He was a man of Travers's own age; a good mixer and a first-rate listener. He had one immediate question to put—whether the job in hand would involve putting off the night's bridge. Not that he minded much, but the Club had better be advised as soon as possible.

"The bridge is the very thing," Travers said. "As a matter of fact the whole scheme depends on your playing tonight. But tell me one thing first. Is it a pretty grim business? I mean, do you look bridge and talk it for three solid hours, or is there anything—well, what I might call social?"

"We'll probably break off somewhere about ten o'clock for a quarter of an hour or so," Faujoie said. "Just a drink and a snack of something."

"Fine," said Travers. "A decent crowd, are they, the people you're playing against? Select and irreproachable?"

"My God, yes!" Faujoie said. "Damn good fellers, of course, but select enough." He gave a quick look. "Why all the preliminary palaver?"

"Sorry," Travers said, "but there's got to be a whole lot of preliminaries. Still, I'd better admit that what you and I are on is the Sonia murder. You regard yourself as co-opted back to the Yard, only the Yard doesn't know it. Now for all the inside information for your private ear."

Tea was over by the time the Colonel had heard the last detail of available information.

"I don't think my brain's functioning," was all the comment he made. "I get the hang of what you've been telling me but I'm damned if I see where I come in."

"You will," Travers told him. "You represent all sorts of things, such as bridge, the society of the wealthy, the owners of country seats and so on. You come in because a certain word happened to stick in my mind—the word *Wryde*. I mean, Lord Wryde with whom you often play bridge."

The Colonel raised his eyebrows.

"I saw his name on the placards the morning after Sonia Vorge was murdered. The actual morning's papers were announcing the murder and the night papers—latest London editions—had the theft of Wryde's famous Romney—*The Earl of Dalhown*. About twenty-five thousand pounds' worth of canvas was stolen from Wryde's town house. Now are you getting any nearer?"

The Colonel grinned. "Just beginning to see."

"Then I'll call your attention to something else," Travers went on. "I rang up certain people just before you came and verified the following. Within the last two years there have been the following thefts of pictures that matter: Titian's *Roman Matron*, Vermeer's *Woman with Two Cavaliers,* and Holbein's *Philosophers*, the last stolen from Admiral Sir Luke Fentrom's house at Bromley."

"Fentrom? I'm playing against him tonight!"

"Better and better," Travers said, and then gave a sad shake of the head. "It's a pity you're going to play so much below form."

"Am I?"

"Of course you are. A man who's had the stroke of luck you've had is bound to be somewhat excited, which is bad for his bridge."

The Colonel grinned again. "Naturally. And what is the stroke of luck?"

"First of all, are you an expert where pictures are concerned?"

"Rather afraid not," the Colonel said.

"Then I'll tell you just as much as you need to know," Travers said. "Too much knowledge might sound suspicious. There were great men after Agamemnon; I mean that a picture needn't be old and fruity to be valuable. Take Dégas, for instance."

"Never heard of him. How's he spell his name?"

"All in good time," Travers said. "His pictures were painted when you and I were in our cradles but a particularly choice example might be worth—well, we won't be too ambitious—say, eight thousand pounds. Your own might actually be worth more. It has no title, of course, but might be called *The Beginner*. It's the usual scene in the wings of a theatre and two ballet dancers are watching a much younger one rehearsing some steps. We'll concoct all the other dope later."

"Carry on," Faujoie said.

"Well, we've arrived at your excitement. Your father bought that picture in Paris years ago and you had it hung in a bedroom; and then, this very morning, a very great man saw it and grew all excited, etc., etc. All you're rather worried about is having the picture in your smoking-room—you brought it down there for him to see—in case the place got burned down. Tomorrow, or Wednesday, you're sending it to the bank, if it hasn't been sold."

"As a matter of fact," Faujoie said, "I *am* getting rather excited. I hope it doesn't play the very devil with my bridge."

"Oh, before I forget it," Travers said. "Were you intending to stay in town tonight?"

"I certainly wasn't."

"Sorry, but you are," Travers said. "What I mean is, that you are and you aren't."

"One of us," said the Colonel, "is mad or tight, and I'm n conscious of being either."

Travers smiled. "Well, so much for the preliminaries. No if you'll grab a sheet of paper, we'll get to work in earnest. The we'll have our first rehearsal."

The Colonel was away by five-thirty. He had intended to sta at the Club and dress there but now a quick trip to his Cockfo ters house was imperative, and after that there was a brief inte view with the Admiral, which Travers was arranging.

That interview was duly arranged and then Travers rang u the Yard. Norris was fetched to the line.

"Sorry to worry you," Travers said, "but were you people s rious last night when you talked of keeping Patrick Carne und observation from then on?"

He could hear that Norris was temporizing.

"Well, sir, we thought if it didn't do any good, it couldn't d any harm."

"Yes, but are you?"

"Well, as a matter of fact, we are, sir." Travers caught th chuckle. "At the moment he's in a club in Piccadilly, and we'v one man at the front and another at the back."

"Hm!" went Travers, in a Whartonian grunt. "Do somethin for me, will you? Call them both off?"

"Call them off, sir!"

"I'll take responsibility," Travers said. "In any case it's onl for tonight, so it can't make all that difference. But do somethin instead. Shift your men to his flat in Sloane Square, and let the take a note of who enters or leaves. If he should go there agai himself and then leave, no matter what time, they're not to fo low him. Have you got that?"

"I'll have to put it up to the Super," Norris told him dubiousl

"As you like," Travers said. "But add a little word from m that if he doesn't agree and things miscarry, then I won't tak the blame."

"What things, sir?"

"You may know tomorrow," Travers said. "If it's all a fiasco, then I'll grovel."

So much for that, he thought, and then began a restless prowling about the room, excited as the Colonel should have been, but wasn't. At the back of his mind was that disturbing thought that a fiasco was only too likely. Yet the Colonel had acted superbly at the rehearsals, with just the right blend of excitement and ignorance. And it was a thundering good scheme, if only nothing went wrong.

But Travers was sure of one thing, that he was far too restless to stay in his own company, especially with five hours of waiting before a move could be made. Then he smiled. Philip Carne, of course! An hour with him might be not unprofitable, now there were all sorts of interesting topics where a mere hint might provoke a reaction. And Philip was on the phone.

But as Travers's hand went to the receiver, it drew back again. Why warn Carne? Better risk his being out, and if he should be in, come on him wholly unawares.

XV
NIGHT LIGHT

PHILIP CARNE opened the door and peered at the figure in the gloom of the landing.

"It's Travers, isn't it?" he said, and at once drew back. "Come in, will you? I take it you want to see me."

That was only his way of speaking, and there was nothing querulous in his tone. But Travers was at once gathering, and the impression was to deepen as the brief talk went on, that Carne was only too ready to receive him, and that Henrietta must have been talking over the phone.

"Won't you let me take your coat?"

"No, don't bother," Travers said. "I'm only staying a moment or two. You're very snug here, by the way."

There was no point in Carne's denying it. The electric fire was on, the chair looked comfortable, and the reading lamp gave a diffused light that was intimate and somehow cozy, while Carne in his flannel hags and blue pullover had a snugness of his own.

"I thought you'd finished writing for a while," Travers remarked with a wave at the manuscript on which Carne apparently had been working.

"Oh, that." He shrugged his shoulders. "Just jotting down some ideas."

"A play, isn't it?" Without his glasses Travers was blind; with them he had a sight that was telescopic.

"Just ideas. It's a man hampered with a neurotic wife and he makes up his mind to kill her."

"Modern?"

"Oh, yes—perfectly. Purely ideas at the moment, as I said. The husband works on his wife's nerves, either to make her commit suicide or to drive her really insane. I might possibly make her kill herself when she is insane, if you follow me."

"And how's he go to work?"

Carne shrugged his shoulders again. "Well, tentatively I've almost decided to make him cut himself while shaving. Then he has the first idea and smears the blood over his throat and comes staggering into the bedroom and pretends he's cut his throat. The same night he'll pretend to talk in his sleep and he'll say he had intended to cut his throat—but lost his nerve—because he's worried about her going mad and how she doesn't know it. Later on the doctor will come to see her—she'll be a hypochondriac, of course—and when he goes out, the husband will pretend to be talking to him outside the door, and the talk—the doctor isn't really there, of course—will be that she's already mad and doesn't know it. That's got to be worked out in considerable detail. It'd be a good scene to have her listening on one side of the door."

"And the climax is when she's actually driven mad?"

Carne frowned. "I'm afraid the climax is in the air."

"Why not make her discover that the husband isn't talking to the doctor after all?" suggested Travers. "Let her discover the scheme, turn the tables and then kill him!"

Carne stared. "My God! that's an idea." He hopped up from the chair and began to pace about the room. "There's something big in this, Travers."

"A bit too raw and meaty for the B.B.C., don't you think?"

"My dear Travers!" Henrietta's very voice was there. "This isn't second-rate rubbish for suburbia; this is a masterpiece."

Travers smiled. "Well, sit down for just one minute while I talk to you about something else." His face straightened. "I promised to keep you informed about developments in the Sonia murder affair."

He was careful to use only the words of the morning's talk at Severns. Carne's air was languid and aloof.

"It's only the guilty who have consciences," he said, and Travers thought at once of that O. Henry story wherein it is proved that when the highbrow is faced with a crisis, he alone resorts to platitudes.

"Well," said Travers, and began preparing for a move, "I thought I'd give you the tip. You, as very well acquainted—in a literary way—with the Montage ghost, might be subject to considerable harrying by the police. My advice—and I hope you'll not be too proud to take it—is to give the police all the help you can, and tell all you know. Make friends, my dear Carne, of the mammon of un-righteousness. Oh, and before I forget it, will you pass on the tip to your brother?"

Philip shot him a look. "But how can he possibly be concerned?"

"Are you your brother's keeper?" said Travers enigmatically, and still in the scriptural vein. "That's a reasonable attitude, I know, but couldn't there be episodes in Patrick's life that even he wouldn't like the police to drag into the light?"

Philip's look was level and frowning. "What do you mean?"

"Nothing," said Travers airily. "But the police have the unhappy knack of uncovering a considerable number of skeletons."

"Very well," he said curtly. "I'll take your advice. Tomorrow, by the way, I'm going down to Severns, and I shall be staying the night. I promised to accompany my mother to some damn village meeting about the coronation. Devastating but unavoidable."

"Well, I won't keep you from work," Travers said. "How are the eyes keeping, by the way?"

"Not so good." He took off his glasses, laid them wearily aside, and rubbed his eyes with his knuckles. "These damned eyes of mine seem to be changing every day. Sometimes I'm rather frightened."

He hooked the glasses on again but Travers was standing by the chair like a man in a dream.

"One good thing though," Carne was going on, "I've seen a man about that nose trouble of mine and he's practically put me right. One very minor operation with a local anesthetic and I shall be normal again." He scrambled to his feet. "Sure you must go?"

"I must," Travers said, and hastily put out a hand. "Don't bother to see me down. Frightfully cold after this room. Good-by, Carne; good-by."

The door closed on him and he hurried down the dark stairs and out to the pavement. As his long strides took him towards Westminster he was trying to assess the importance of the strange thing he had seen, and to fit it into its essential place. Then a crawling taxi caught his eye and in five minutes he was entering the Yard, and whom should he run into but George Wharton.

"The very man I want," Wharton said. "I've been trying to get you on the phone the last half-hour. Come in here a minute and let's clear things up."

Travers got his blow in first.

"If it's about the men who're watching Patrick Carne's flat then I'd be grateful if you could see your way clear to calling them off altogether for just a couple of nights. The fact is, I don't want him scared."

"What is all this?" Wharton asked. "Something you've discovered on your own?"

Travers hunted desperately for a lie of the most spotless white, and found one just in time.

"Just something that happened to come my way. You see he's a bridge expert, which means gambling generally—don'

ou agree? He plays till all hours at various clubs and then it's
uite likely that he goes along to some questionable place or
ther: a private house run as a gambling den, for instance. What
might be able to do is to prove he was in such a place at the
ital time on the night of the murder."

"I get you," Wharton said. "The trouble is he doesn't want to
ive away the ones who're running this shady club."

"Something of the sort. But if he has the idea the police are
n his tail, he might think it's because of the night-club place
nd all sorts of other alibis might get faked. He may even own
he place himself."

"You carry on," Wharton said. "Tell me his alibi's good and
ve'll wipe him off the list. I'll see the men are called off."

"One minute," Travers said. "I'm going to put something up
o you. Philip Carne is going to Severns some time tomorrow
nd he's escorting his mother to a coronation meeting in the vil-
age. Would it be possible for you to be there when they return
iome, and question the pair of them, in the same room at the
ame time?"

Wharton frowned. "What's the idea? Collusion?"

"Even that's not improbable," Travers said. "But if each
acks up the other's alibi, then you know only too well that they
night as well be wiped off the list. I'm not dreaming of telling
ou your business or teaching you how to go to work, but I do
eel that if you apologized for seeing them and said it was really
he last time they'd be troubled,then you could hear them back
ach other up. I'd like to know every minute detail of their two
libis and how each confirms the other."

"But we have that information."

"But not obtained in the way I suggest. Each does depend on
he other, George. You've heard them separately but not dove-
ailed in. Besides, I've discovered something rather suspicious
bout Philip."

Wharton's eyes opened at once.

"I've just come from his flat," Travers said, "and while I was
here he thought it necessary to tell me how bad his eyesight
vas; and by way of illustration he took off his glasses and rubbed

his tired eyes. But he laid his glasses down on some manuscrip
I was standing clean over it and I could read the writing on th
manuscript paper clean through the glasses!"

"The glasses are fakes?"

"Undoubtedly. The writing wasn't the least bit distorted."

Wharton pursed out his lips, then gave a little smile.

"The old game of swank, that's what it is. He took to glasse
because it made him look more interesting. Isn't that the kind c
bloke you told me he was?"

Travers made a wry face.

"That's it for a fiver," Wharton went on. "Take the case c
Harold Lloyd and the films, for instance. They tell me his glasse
aren't glasses at all—only rims!" He chuckled to himself, the
sobered down. "Still, I'll certainly do as you suggest, and ru
down to Severns tomorrow night. Anything else happened?"

"No," said Travers, and thought. "Henrietta's as unscrupu
lous as I feared. I'm sure she repeated to Philip all the suppose
confidences I'd imparted to her this morning."

"Close in together, those two, are they?" He nodded grimly
"Well, we'll hear what they've got to say for themselves tomo
row night. Now, if you'll excuse me, I'll call off those men from
Sloane Square."

Travers dismissed from his mind that curious affair of Phil
ip Carne and the glasses, not because he believed in Wharton'
ingenious objections to any sinister motive, but because his ow
opinions had set going a train of thought. And new thoughts wer
dangerous in view of what lay before him in the next few hours.

He made a good meal when he reached the flat, for ther
was no telling when another meal would come along. Then h
changed into a dark suit and it was half-past nine when he en
tered the Tube station. At the other end he walked the mile and
half to Faujoie's house, and it was then eleven o'clock. The house
hold was in bed but Youngs, the Colonel's man, was waiting.

He was an old sapper, like his master, and he reported tha
the buzzer was rigged up in the shrubbery that lay both sides c
the front entrance. There was no need for an intruder to scal
the garden walls with their broken-glass tops, for the main gat

was left unlocked and there was no public lighting within half a mile. Then Travers was taken to the house and shown the lie of the land.

"I'll sit over this telephone," Travers said, "and you get back to your peep-hole. And don't forget. Whoever it is, you're not to follow. Just sound the buzzer and wait for these lights to go on. Then you can come running."

Just before half-past eleven the phone went.

"We've finished earlier than we thought," Colonel Faujoie said. "I think everything was swallowed all right, but of course I couldn't see his face. Now I'm off ostensibly to visit a certain select night-club with the Admiral. Be with you inside half an hour."

Travers sat on in the dark and waited. Just after midnight there was the sound of a key in the lock of the side-door, and in stepped Faujoie.

"Left the car well out of his way," he whispered. "Everything set? If so we'd better take up stations. He's liable to travel as fast as I did."

The curtains of the smoking-room window had been drawn along the wall, and he disappeared behind them. Travers was outside the door, ready to squeeze flat against the wall alongside a tall grandfather clock. That clock ticked solemnly on, and the sleeping house seemed to roar with its reverberations when it struck the half-hour. Then it ticked on and on, and suddenly there was the low throbbing of the buzzer.

Travers's heart gave a leap forward, and his ears were strained to listen. Still there was no sound but the clock. Ten minutes went by and it was by chance that he caught the flicker of a light at the far end of the hall where he stood. From floor to walls it was traveling, and like a flash he nipped inside the smoking-room door, and with a warning whisper to Faujoie, crouched behind the end of a settee.

The clock struck the hour and before the sound had died, there was a circle of light on the wall across the room. It moved towards the window, then there was the faintest shuffle of feet. Travers rose and his hand went to the switch. The lights of the room flashed full on.

"Stand fast, Carne!"

Faujoie stepped from the curtains and Travers closed in from the door. Patrick Carne stood motionless, eyes coolly surveying Faujoie, then his head swiveled and his narrowing eyes took in Travers. Feet were heard in the hall and Youngs was at the door.

"Got a gun of any sort, Carne?" asked the Colonel.

"Oh, no," Carne told him indifferently.

"Give us your word you won't try to bolt?"

"Why shouldn't I?"

"You'll be in a damn bad way if you do try any monkey-tricks," Faujoie told him. "Youngs, you lock that door and stand outside with the key. How'd he get in, by the way?"

"Through the lower hall window, sir."

"Good enough," the Colonel said. He drew the curtains again, then waved Carne to a chair. "Sit down there, Carne. We three are going to have a little chat."

"We're going to put a strange proposition up to you, Carne," Travers began. "We've only to speak a few words over the phone and that's the end of you. You might get away with five years, but it'd be the end of you."

Carne nodded as if none too interested.

"What we propose," went on Travers, "is that you should sign a confession, to include the taking of certain other pictures—a Vermeer, a Titian and a Holbein—"

"Sorry," Carne said, "but there's nothing doing. I might have been concerned in the—er—transaction that had to do with two of them, but the Titian was nothing to do with me."

"We're prepared to take your word for that," Faujoie said. "Now perhaps you'd like to hear the general drift of the confession."

"Not interested," Carne said again. "What I want to know is where's the catch. I'm throwing in my hand, but not to that extent."

"The catch is your uncle," Travers told him dryly. "If you're up on this present and other charges, his name is bound to crop up too. What's the truth about him, by the way? He must have known the history and ownership of those pictures?"

"I think perhaps he did," Carne said reflectively. "The trouble was when he went mad over that collection of his. He's got the idea of making it absolutely unique. It doesn't matter where they come from so long as he has them. He gloats over them. Sometimes he'll sit for hours in front of one."

"Sonia was in it, of course?"

"Maybe."

"And your brother Philip?"

That woke him up. "You keep Philip out of this. He never was in it."

"Then how do you account for the fact that he knew?"

Carne gave him a long look.

"Suppose he did know. I'm telling you that he took no part whatever. If you'll admit the remark as confidential, I'll even admit that he tried to induce me to drop out. He did that again the very morning after I'd taken that Romney." He smiled ironically. "You're getting your confession, you see?"

"Well, our terms are these," Faujoie said. "In order to save the tremendous scandal, and because we're of the honest opinion that your uncle is not mentally responsible for his part in the robberies, we're prepared to do this. You'll take this morning's six o'clock plane to France. Within two days those pictures which you know for a certainty have been come by crookedly will be sent to Scotland Yard. Do that how you like. You may even pretend it was all a joke if you like. But if the pictures are not back, and if you ever attempt again to set foot in this country, then Travers and I are free, and we tell all we know to you-know-whom."

It was half-past two before that confession was drawn up and signed and countersigned. Then Faujoie produced plain paper and envelopes.

"Better write your resignations to your clubs. If you wish to write to your mother, you must leave it open for us to see. When that's done we'll move on to your flat."

It was half-past three when the Colonel's car drew into Sloane Square. Youngs stayed with the car and the two went into the flat with Carne.

"Tell me something before you begin your packing," Travers said. "How did you work that wireless and clatter stunt that made your neighbor think you were in here when you weren't?"

"Comic business with kettle and string," Carne said, and left it at that.

"And just one other thing. On the night of the twentieth of March, when you were not here, Sonia was here."

"Why not?" he said. "I gave her the free run of this place. She was often bored enough with her own."

"The wireless went on after she came in," Travers said, "and a man's voice was heard. Will you tell us who the man was?"

"A man?" His cheek flushed with a quick anger. "You're wrong. She wasn't the sort to do that kind of thing."

"And suppose I'm not wrong?"

He shrugged his shoulders. "Do as you damn please. I'm not interested. I will say this, though. If the wireless was on, then it might have been some crooner or other. Or what about a play? They have music with plays, don't they?"

He went through to do his packing and the two were left by themselves. Faujoie whispered.

"Can't believe it's gone off like this. There must be a snag somewhere."

Travers shook his head. "Wait till it's over, then we'll have a yarn."

Faujoie made no bones about searching Carne's two bags before they were strapped, and it was half-past four when the car set off again. Carne bought his own ticket and said a word or two before he mounted the plane.

"Afraid I rather underestimated you, Travers. Decent of you though, and you too, Colonel."

A nod and he was going. The two watched till the plane was heading southeast, then Travers heaved a sigh.

"Well, thank heaven he's gone. Every minute I was expecting something to go wrong."

"You don't look any too cheerful now," the Colonel said. "What about some coffee to liven us up?"

So they had early breakfast in the restaurant, and in the middle of it Travers caught the other's eye, and both of them smiled.

"We might just as well say it," Travers said. "We're thinking the same thing. If a word of this gets out, we'll be had up for compounding a felony, hindering the course of justice, aiding and abetting—"

"I know. Everything, bar shooting game without a license, and they may have us up for that. Still, I'm not letting it worry me."

"It isn't only that," Travers said. "We planned just a bit too quickly. We've hustled Carne out of England, but that won't stop him telephoning wherever he likes when he lands at Paris."

"Telephoning?" Then he nodded. "I get you. I've been wondering just what this night's business had to do with the murder."

"It may have a lot to do with it," Travers said. "It eliminates Patrick Carne as the murderer, and to that extent it makes even more precarious the position of any suspect who's left." He leaned forward and his voice lowered. "You're pretty deep in this now, so I'll put something up to you. Certain members of his family were aware that Patrick was in that picture-stealing line. Patrick was a long way from a fool, as we both know, so why shouldn't he in his turn have been aware of the identity of the murderer? If he is, then the first thing he'll do will be to put that murderer on his guard, and above all to warn him against myself. I don't claim that anything I can do is likely to help the police overmuch, but I am claiming that as far as actually taking any further hand is concerned, I might as well stay here the rest of my life and live on cold ham and coffee."

"You never know," the Colonel told him with a sideways, optimistic nod. "And where do we go when we leave here?"

"I'd rather like to get home," Travers said. "And if I'm none too communicative on the road, it'll be because I'm working out some yarn or other for George Wharton. Which reminds me. You'll have to be included too."

* * *

It was after eight when Travers came in, and never had he felt so bleary-eyed. The first thing he did was to ring the Yard and it was Norris with whom he got into touch.

"Everything's worked out well," Travers said. "Patrick Carne's alibi can be warranted sound for that Wednesday night There's no doubt about it, Norris. I can vouch for it myself, and so can someone whose name'd surprise you if I told you."

"He's definitely out then, sir?"

"Very definitely," Travers said. "And before I forget it, will you note that I have a private job of work I must attend to today so don't ring me as I shan't be available."

In ten minutes that private job of work had begun, for Travers was sound asleep in his bed. It was nearly six o'clock that evening when Palmer thought it as well to wake him.

XVI
ATTACK FROM THE REAR

TRAVERS had a bath, donned the dark brown suit which Palmer laid out, and, as he took the first sip of a sherry, told himself that he had never felt fitter in his life. The brain was functioning too, for no sooner did he settle into his chair than a whole series of illuminating ideas presented themselves.

In less than a moment he knew himself on the edge of something vital, and for fear some connecting link should escape and baffle him, he fetched a sheet of paper and jotted the ideas down. Soon they made a sequence, and when the time had come to re-assess them and write in their inevitable order, he knew that an astounding discovery had been made. Everything depended on the extent to which Patrick Carne had told the truth. If they were lies about Philip's attempts to reform him—or warn him off the game—then the new theory was untenable. But Travers was sure there was truth in Patrick's statements about Philip and that he had not been merely shielding him in some clumsy, extempore way.

Assume then that Philip Carne was aware that after the death of Trove Patrick had become Sonia's close ally in that providing of the raw picture material which should extract considerable sums from mad old Sir Raphael. From whom could he have obtained that information if not from Sonia herself; Sonia who had chosen him as the man of her moment and who would make no bones about disclosing anything? From that it was reasonable to deduce that Patrick had lied when he said that no man had been with Sonia in the Sloane Square flat on the night of the twentieth of March. Philip had been there, and it was there and elsewhere that Sonia and Philip had worked out the details of that scheme to get Sidley's money and then be rid of him and make a fool of him at the same time—a scheme that would have appealed enormously to Philip, who hated Sidley like poison.

Then Sonia was murdered and the following morning Philip rang up Patrick with two pieces of information which he had gathered ostensibly from the papers—that Patrick had been up to his tricks again and taken the Romney, and that Sonia was dead. "For God's sake chuck that game for good and all," Philip would have said. "You're bound to get caught in the long run, and think what effect that'll have on the lot of us, and mother not the least. Sonia's dead and that gives you your chance. Put that damn picture in the fire and to hell with it. I've told you the same thing before and you've gone your own way."

Now such action on the part of Philip established the fact that Philip knew well enough that Patrick had not killed Sonia. Was it less reasonable to assume that Patrick must have suspected at once that it was Philip who had done the killing? If so, then already Patrick would have rung up Philip from somewhere in France to put him on his guard. That perhaps mattered little. If Philip had indeed done the killing, then he would have taken his own precautions.

Then all at once the hackneyed words flashed across Travers's mind, about tangled webs woven by those who practice to deceive. The action which he and Faujoie had thought best to take would make it impossible for Wharton to be told a word of the new theory. If a case were to be made out against Philip Carne as the murderer, then a new series of motives would have to be found. "Very well," said Travers to himself, "the only thing to do is to find those motives. In the long run I may have to own up to Wharton, but in the meantime, no more lies."

And the more he thought, the more he was convinced that Philip had done that murder. If every angel and archangel vouched for his alibi, then somehow he must have swindled the hosts of heaven, and he was still the murderer. And as for swindling, what about those fake glasses? Travers's mind ran quickly back to that evening in the Sophocles, when he had first been aware that Philip wore glasses at all. Carne had been just a bit too talkative about the eyes and too anxious for advice. Yet it was just like him to take any way of calling attention to himself, and Travers frowned as he thought of that and as the balance swung from side to side.

Then another idea came—the day after Sonia's murder. Just what should have happened? The dirty trick having been duly played on Sidley, he himself should have lunched with Sonia, and a third person. All most ironic it would have been. Patrick would have been the third, and he would have brought that Romney with him. After a suitable outpouring of her grievances—all highly amusing—she would have flown that picture to the South of France, having first set the ball rolling in the matter of a separation.

Travers made a note of that, glanced at the clock, then folded the paper and put it carefully into his inner pocket. Then he became aware of something else, and he took it out. It was the envelope containing what he had assumed to be the hairs from a cat but what he now thought were those from a Belgian hare. Then again he was frowning to himself as he fingered them. From what he was remembering of rabbits and Belgian hares in his own school-boy days, their fur was shortish and more fine in texture. Then all at once he was getting to his feet and ringing for Palmer.

"I'm just slipping along to Ayres Buildings, back of the Strand," he said. "That oughtn't to take more than a quarter of an hour, so will you hold back dinner till then?"

It was a vet of his acquaintance whom Travers was propos-
ng to see, and he was lucky enough to find him in. Travers pro-
uced the envelope and solemnly explained his difficulty. Chim-
ley, the vet, took one look and then made a wry face.

"Nothing like it, my dear fellow."

"What about cat fur then?"

Chimpley shook his head again, fingered the hairs, held
hem to the light, and frowned. Then he smiled.

"I think I've got it. Would you mind waiting here for a min-
te?"

Travers heard him calling in the corridor. The voice might
ecede with the steps but the words were distinct enough.

"Ho Ling! . . . Ho Ling!"

"Funny," said Travers to himself. "Whoever'd have thought
hat Chimpley kept a Chinese man-servant!"

It was not till an hour later that Travers came home again,
nd who should be waiting for him but George Wharton.

"Here you are then," Wharton said. "I'd made up my mind to
ive you two more minutes, then I was going."

Travers was still staring. "But what about the interview?"

Wharton grimaced. "I thought I'd use a little more tact.
People don't want to talk after being at a meeting. Philip would
e there for dinner, I said to myself, so I rolled up at half-past
ix. Said I wouldn't keep them five minutes and it'd be for the
ast time."

"And it worked?"

"Worked?" He snorted. "They were all over me—that's the
nly thing that's made me do a bit of thinking. That old hag
night have been my own aunt. Affable wasn't the word. He was
s nervy as hell but just as polite. And talk about fitting in! They
ad everything worked out to the last split second."

"Collusion?"

Wharton glared. "I didn't say so, did I? And what's the good
f it is? They can prove by each other's evidence that neither of
hem left the house at the time we want. That wipes all inquiry
ff the slate. Unless we can find a couple of witnesses to swear

they identified either of them elsewhere, then as far as we're concerned, both the Carnes were where they say they were."

"You may as well have a bite now you're here," Travers said. "We'll talk and eat at the same time."

"Can't spare the time," Wharton said. "Five minutes and I must be gone. But don't let me stop you."

"Then if you don't mind I think I'll make a start," Travers said, and rang for dinner. "Now tell me about the alibis."

"Exact times don't matter," Wharton said, "but she says he came to bed at eleven. She hadn't a watch or clock in her room but she now professes to remember she heard a downstairs clock strike the hour. After that she heard him get into bed; she heard him snore; she heard him wake, so to speak, and move about the room; and she heard suspicious sounds from outside. At just after midnight—she says it wasn't more than ten past—Philip knocked at her door, and the rest of that you know. His tale corroborates hers. He went up to bed at about eleven, fell asleep at once, woke and heard suspicious noises, heard his mother stirring in her room, dozed off again, woke just before midnight and thought he heard his mother again, then got up and knocked at her door." Wharton waved his hands. "That's about the lot. If it doesn't let out the pair of them, my name's not what it is."

"It certainly looks like it," Travers said.

"I tell you they've got it all cut and dried," Wharton went on. "He says he went to the window and looked out? Very well, then she heard him go to the window. And the thing that gets my goat is that I know there's something fishy. I know it by her manner and his. No more of that supercilious touch from her. It's *Superintendent* this way and *Superintendent* that way, and she swearing like blazes that dear Philip did just what she heard him do. His line was to reinforce what she said, and put in a word for her side of the alibi." He shook his head. "Still, I'm not unjust and I'm not prejudiced. Their alibis may be right and they may not. The great thing is we shall never prove they're not. What's more, I lay that inside the week they prime one of the maids to remember something."

Travers's second course came in and Wharton got up to go.

"Some time tomorrow there'll have to be a conference," he said. "Patrick Carne's out of it, so I understand, and now the other two. Cordovan was out long ago, and Coales's wife will swear he couldn't have had a thing to do with it. Who's left, I don't know. Maybe you or me murdered her if only we could work it out."

"Now you're getting bitter," Travers said, and laid his napkin aside to accompany him to the door. "But I've got a hunch, George. I'm prepared to bet a new hat that you're in a brighter mood this time tomorrow night."

Wharton stopped short. "Oh? Why do you think that?"

"Just a hunch," Travers said. "Alibis have been bust before."

"Not this kind," Wharton said. Then his lips pursed. "You're not working out some comic contraption with a kettle and a bit of string?"

Travers smiled. "Now you're being bitter again. Haven't you ever made a bad shot, George, that you reproach me with mine?"

Wharton dismissed the question with a grunt and stepped into the lift.

"Where can I catch you first thing in the morning?" Travers called through the bars.

"I shall be at the Yard at seven," Wharton told him. "And that'll be long before you're up."

Travers beamed at him as the lift began to descend, but no sooner was it out of sight than he was sprinting back to his meal.

"I was just taking it away to keep it warm, sir," Palmer said.

"Leave everything as it is," Travers told him. "Grab a hat and coat and get the car round as quickly as you can. I'll put out all lights."

Five minutes later the Rolls was moving off towards the Strand. Travers kept to his thirty statutory miles and when he exceeded it, hoped for the best. But the roads were clear and they made good time to Lewisham, and after that the car began to travel. A quarter of a mile from Severns, Travers drew the car up by a field gate. Palmer hopped out and opened it and the Rolls was backed into the meadow. The time was then nine o'clock.

"We shan't want the torch," Travers said, with a glance at the new moon. "We haven't seen a soul about, and that's a good sign. We're gambling on that coronation meeting lasting more than an hour."

He crammed the small sack into his overcoat pocket and the two moved off towards Severns. It was a lightish night but they hugged the shadowed side of the lane, and once, when a courting couple passed them, halted and pretended to be deep in talk. Then just short of the entrance to Philip Carne's garage, Travers issued his orders.

"You stay here, Palmer, and if you see the lights of a car coming up that hill, let out a whistle. You *can* whistle, can't you?"

"An accomplishment of my younger days, sir."

His fingers went to his mouth. Travers grabbed his arm.

"My God! don't try it now." A last whisper and he was off. "Don't forget then. Whistle if a car comes and then move of back to the Rolls."

Inside three minutes he was back and in the small sack was the straw from the hutch. The rain had helped there. But for that Hughes would have burnt it; as it was it was still heavy with wet. Two hundred yards along the lane Palmer looked back.

"The lights of a car, sir."

"Right," said Travers. "Then we'll wait here in the hedge and see if it stops on the way."

A second or two and the car had stopped. A dark figure was seen, then the headlights swiveled as the car moved inside the drive.

"Another coronation meeting over," Travers said, and stepped out to the lane again. "A very patriotic gentleman, Palmer, the one who owns that car."

"Indeed, sir?" Palmer said.

"Yes," said Travers reminiscently. "Has a color scheme of red and white daisies along his drive, and what's worrying me is that I'm afraid I rather trod on some of them. Red and white daisies, Palmer, edged with blue lobelia. You get the idea?"

"Coronation colors, sir."

"Exactly! The gentleman was so anxious to have them that he made his gardener fetch them from the nursery. Now you take this sack and heave it in the back of the car when I've undone the gate."

At a quarter past ten that night the table of Travers's dining-room had been cleared and news-papers were spread on it. Then Travers emptied out the straw from the sack.

"I won't apologize for being mad," he said amusedly to Palmer, "because you've been keeping the secret for years."

Palmer smiled, being used to Travers's jokes.

"So draw up the port decanter for yourself," Travers went on, "and the whiskey and soda for me, then we'll get to work. I hope it won't be an all-night sitting."

With the hairs from the envelope for guide they began a patient examination of each individual straw, and at half-past eleven when the first hair was found, the two beamed at each other. It was a quarter past twelve when the second turned up.

"You push off to bed." Travers said, "and I'll carry on."

But Palmer was too interested to abandon the hunt. Coffee was brewed and at three o'clock the total of hairs was five.

"Good enough," said Travers. "Now I'll write out a statement for you to sign and we'll put these five hairs in an envelope and seal it, and you can sign that too. After that I think we might as well turn in. And if you could anyhow give me a knock at about six in the morning, I'd be very much obliged. Breakfast can wait till you're ready."

At six the same morning Travers put on his glasses and his dressing gown and made for the phone. Wharton was called at his private number, and in two minutes the General's voice was heard.

"Hallo?"

"Travers speaking, George. I want to put something up to you."

"A bit early, aren't you?"

"Yes, we're catching an early worm. Got a sheet of paper? Right, then take down this, or perhaps you'll remember it. You ready? . . . Well, I want you to go to Severns. Leave your car well out of sight and when you come within two hundred yards you'll see a meadow with a chestnut wood on the right. You'll have field-glasses and from the wood you'll be able to look down on Philip Carne's garage. I'd like you to be there not later than eight o'clock."

Wharton grunted. "What's in the wind?"

"Too long to explain," Travers told him, "but it's more than important. But there's something else. Have two men on motor-bikes each at a little distance from the house to pick him up and follow him whichever way he goes. He'll probably make for quiet, open country and then he'll stop. Try to discover what he does. He may have been digging, for example, and if so there'll be freshly turned earth somewhere in the neighborhood of where he stops. Find it and when you know what he's buried, get back to Sevenoaks as quickly as you can and phone me from there. I'll be sitting here waiting. Now would you mind repeating?"

Wharton duly repeated. Travers added a rider.

"I'm relying on your being in your peep-hole at eight o'clock, George. Sorry to be so mysterious but there's no time to explain."

"This isn't any kettle and string business?"

"It's urgent, George; damnably urgent."

There was a silence for a moment, then, "Right!" said Wharton laconically, and rang off.

Travers dressed leisurely and by seven o'clock had finished breakfast. Then he got to work in earnest. First he rang up a typewriting agency whom he frequently employed and asked if a reliable shorthand man could be sent round at not later than a quarter to eight. Palmer, the flat electrician, began constructing a rough-and-ready extension to the receiver. Then at half-past seven the phone bell went—Wharton ringing from Sevenoaks.

"Thought I'd let you know we're on the way," he said. "I ought to be lying doggo by eight or before."

The stenographer arrived and Travers began a rehearsal. The number that Travers rang was to be recorded and each

ord of the conversation taken down, together with descrip-
ive adjectives of the tone of the voice at the other end. Eight
'clock drew slowly near and at last Travers gave a last look
ound to see that everything was set, then rang up Severns.
hilip Carne's voice answered.

"Hallo?"

"Is that you, Carne?" Travers's voice was quick and urgent.
Travers speaking. Wharton was down at your place last night?"

"Yes, but—"

"Don't talk, Carne—listen. That was all a blind. The police
re after you!"

"After *me!*"

(Wearily) "For God's sake, Carne, don't talk! They know
hat you've buried in that shrubbery!" He heard the quick
reath. "I can't say more. I daren't. I'm just giving you the tip.
re you there?"

A faint sound told that Carne was still there.

"Listen, Carne. Get it away, do you hear? Get it away. Then
et back to town as soon as you can. I'll try and ring you again
rom here. . . . Sorry. Daren't say another word. Do as I say and
ou may be all right. And if you don't believe me, look for the
traw that was in the hutch."

Travers hung up and then let out a deep breath. Then a
yped copy was made of the one-sided conversation, and signed
nd witnessed.

"Palmer will get you some breakfast," Travers told the ste-
ographer. "If you've had some, then have some more. Then
rab some of these books and amuse yourself in the kitchen till
omething turns up."

Next Travers dialled the Yard. Norris was not in but an ur-
ent message was left. At nine, Norris rang.

"Listen, Norris," Travers said. "This order is as from Super-
ntendent Wharton. Have two good men, one at back and one
t front, put on Philip Carne's flat in Victoria, and see they're
icely hidden away. Have a spare man if necessary and keep
hem there till further orders."

"Right, sir. And what're they to do when they're there?"

Travers smiled. "Sorry, Norris. I'm just a bit flustered this morning. They're to report when he enters his flat and they're to tail him wherever he goes when he leaves it."

Peace descended on the flat. Travers read the *Times* and tried to tell himself that the words were not blurred. Ten o'clock came, and at a quarter past, Norris rang to say that Philip Carne had just garaged the car and entered his flat. His manner was very agitated.

Another quarter of an hour went by, then there was the sound of the lift. Quick feet were in the corridor, there was a tap at the door, and in came Wharton.

"Couldn't ring from Sevenoaks," he said. "I'd have had to go back. Want me to bring in what we've dug up?"

"Just a minute first," Travers said. "Tell me what happened."

"He was at the garage at five past eight," Wharton said, "and he came running. He looked round for something all among the shrubs and bushes but I couldn't see what. Then he dug something up and put it in a sack, and smoothed the ground over with a rake, working like hell all the time. Then he got out his car and off he went. One of my men was on him and went past his car not far from Montage, drawn up by the road near a little wood in a lane. I was warned and came along after he'd gone. We found where he'd been digging. I ought to have told you he took a spade with him when he bolted." He shot a look from under his grizzled eyebrows. "I suppose you know what we dug up?"

"Yes," said Travers. "A fawn-colored Pekinese dog." He shook his head. "A bit gamy, wasn't it?"

"It wasn't any too fresh," Wharton said. "That's why I left it downstairs."

"Take your coat off," Travers said, and made for the phone. Then he swerved away to the kitchen and called in the stenographer.

"I'm ringing up Carne," he explained to Wharton, "and the talk is being taken down. Carne got back to his flat some time ago." He thought of something. "Any particular name to that place where you dug up the dog?"

"Carter's Wood," Wharton said. "I asked at a farm where it belonged."

All was set and Travers dialed Philip Carne's number. When he spoke his voice was even more tense and urgent.

"That you, Carne? Travers speaking. I've just had the tip that the police know where you bought that dog, and why!"

A little laugh came from Carne's end, but there was something deeper than anxiety in it.

"But look here, Travers—"

"For God's sake, Carne, don't talk. There's no time for it. Don't try to bluff me. It's the police you've got to bluff. I tell you they're after you. After you—do you hear! . . . How do I know? I can't tell you. But if you still don't believe me, then what about the rope?"

He strained to listen but there was only that same faint sound. His own voice became even more urgent.

"Are you there? I'm ringing off now. I'll get what news I can and let you know."

Another deep breath was let out and he turned to Wharton. Wharton spoke first.

"And where did he get the dog?"

"Don't know," said Travers. "That was a bluff."

"And that bit about the rope?"

Travers shook his head. "That was a bluff too."

XVII
SURRENDER

WHARTON SAW ALL Travers's exhibits and documents, and still confessed himself as very much in the dark. What was the idea, for instance, of ringing Carne up and tipping him off about the police?

"I owe you more than an explanation, George," Travers said. "I think you've been very lenient with me. For me to have had the audacity to ask a Scotland Yard Superintendent to get behind a hedge with a pair of field-glasses—"

Wharton was clapping him on the shoulder.

"That's all right. I know you and you know me—so it seems. Still, there're a lot of things I'd like to know."

"Then I'll put just one question," Travers said. "Are you still convinced, even with the extra knowledge, that you could never bring a case against Philip Carne?"

Wharton pursed his lips. "I am. I still say his alibi is unshakeable. One proviso, though. If his mother doesn't lose her nerve."

Travers smiled dryly. "That's about as likely as your entering a monastery."

"Just a minute," Wharton said. "I'm beginning to see things. The other one might lose his nerve. Isn't that it? You've got hold of certain information that doesn't upset his alibi and you're trying to bluff him into thinking you have more."

"That's it," Travers said. "A flank attack, George; and we know more than you think."

"And what if he keeps his nerve and won't he bluffed?"

Travers shrugged his shoulders. "Then we lose. All the same, I think it's our one chance. What's more, I think that what he's done this morning—and what he's said—shows his nerve is weakening."

Wharton frowned. "Yes, he's in that flat. Back and front watched and he doesn't know it. All the suspense to himself, and we playing with him like a cat with a mouse." He whipped round. "Suppose his alibi's sound, and he's laughing at us?"

Travers shrugged his shoulders again. "Then there's no harm done. We've everything to gain and nothing to lose."

Wharton grunted. "If he does lose his nerve, what'll he do? Bolt?"

"I imagine so," Travers said. "He'll stay in his flat to get the tips I'm passing on to him till the time comes to make a decision. We can determine the time but I'd say he'd be more likely to bolt when it's dark."

"I'll stay on here for a bit," Wharton said, and drew himself a chair to the fire. "You get on and tell me everything you know."

Travers came back from the bookshelves with a slim, paper-bound volume.

"Put this in your pocket and dip into it when you have time. I've marked one special thing—*Pink Pearls*. Just one of a series of one-act plays in the Elizabethan manner, which was published for Carne a year or so ago."

Wharton looked suspicious. "I haven't got to read all his damn books, have I?"

Travers smiled. "Not exactly, George. But I'll tell you about Pink Pearls, because I think it has a bearing not only on him but also on the case. It's a play in blank verse—rather fine verse, even if somewhat luscious. Scene—Venice. Ducal lover sees his rival leave the mistress's house. The Duke then enters. Beautiful lady receives him; passionate embraces and all the rest of it, and he doesn't let on that he's being double-crossed. Then she asks if he's brought the necklace of pink pearls he'd promised. He says he has and if she closes her eyes he'll put them round her neck. He does it but the pearls are not pink and she flies in a temper. He cajoles her, gets her in a reasonable frame of mind and then, while they embrace, suddenly cuts her throat. As she dies with horror in her eyes, he looks down at the pearls and laughs. The blood from her throat had stained them. 'Pink Pearls,' he says, and laughs again as the curtain falls."

Wharton glared. "Sounds indecent to me. People have been locked up for writing stuff like that."

"I told the story very crudely," Travers said. "All the same I think you can put it with the other things I've told you about Philip Carne. It does help to show the kind of mind he has. And now to get on with this actual case. The first part is pure supposition.

"First, we must guess at motives. We'll say that Sonia fell madly in love with him and that he found her very attractive for a time and then began to get very tired. Rather frightened too, perhaps. She was expecting marriage and he certainly never intended tying himself to her for what might have been life. Also, if she were dead and Sidley was hanged for her murder, then Sir Raphael's money would ultimately come to himself—or most of it would. That's enough, I think, for motive."

"Damn the motives," said Wharton. "I don't care *why* he did it. What I want to hear from you is *whether* he did it, and how."

"We're coming to that," Travers said. "But we must agree that Sonia went pretty far with him. The trouble about marriage was that both she and Carne were hard up, and then Sidley began chasing her again and she and Carne between them evolved that scheme for getting his money and then turning him down. Out of that came Carne's murder scheme, which we'll leave for a bit. Meanwhile his policy was to keep her on the end of a string. He agreed to do all she suggested.

"So much for supposition. Now we come to facts—"

"Which is what I've been waiting for," said Wharton patiently.

"Here they are then," Travers told him. "You mayn't regard them as facts, but I do. They concern his alibi and how he faked it. He may have got the idea first by working out one of his thrillers, or it may have arisen out of the dog. He saw or was told of a Pekinese which snored. All Pekinese do that, and some snore in very human ways. Where he bought the dog will be for you people to find out, but the dog's a fact and we know it. Also I say that at first the murder scheme didn't depend on Montage Court. It could have been worked at Sonia's flat. Montage Court, when she suggested it for *her* scheme, fitted only too well with his.

"He bought the Pekinese then. I saw one yesterday, a dog called Ho Ling, that's probably the very spit of the one you just dug up, and its owner tells me it snores like an old man. Philip kept the dog in his Bloomsbury flat and learned to imitate its snore. When his mother remarked one day that he had snored terribly, he said, 'So I've been told. It's all on account of my illness. But I'm not down very often and I don't think it will disturb you. If it does, we can easily have other rooms.' I may say that when the snore had become an established fact, he later tried it out on me, doubtless because he knew I was a hireling of the Yard. He also took good care to let me know about his eyes, the idea being that there're certain things a man with bad eyes can't do. I fell for that later when I assumed he couldn't have been the ghost.

"Another piece of preparation by his elaborate and ingenious mind was the assumption of the character of Stavangel, and setting abroad the rumor that Trove was alive. Trove, if alive, would later have been made out by Carne to have been the murderer. And now to the night of the murder."

Wharton stirred in his chair at that.

"Carne drove his own car to Severns and he arrived after the gardener had gone home. He put the dog in a hutch in the garage and knew it wouldn't bark. If it did or if it snored, no one would hear because the garage is well away from the house. Then he dug a small grave in the shelter of the shubbery.

"After his mother had gone to bed he took out her car. Two ways are open—one uphill and one down. He ran the car downhill and left it well away from the house. Then he brought the dog to his bedroom, a room that his mother was never allowed to enter. If the dog barked, then no particular harm would be done. She would say next morning that she had heard a dog in his room, and he would admit it and say it was a surprise present for her. Immediately after the murder, by the way, he pretended a great horror of dogs.

"But the dog did not bark. Pekes rarely do when they're in a room that has the smell of their masters. He had faked the clock and it was much earlier than eleven. I should say he was at Montage by eleven. What happened there, we'll leave, and return with him to Severns. If the clock that Henrietta heard strike had been changed, then it might have been twenty minutes past twelve. He came home the other way this time, so that the car could free-wheel down into its garage. Then he nipped up to his room and strangled the dog. Then he knocked at his mother's door and mentioned noises and said he'd go down and investigate. Down he went and buried the dog, and changed the lock of his garage for the filed one. In the morning, with Hughes not coming till after nine o'clock, he could have a look round by daylight. The last thing he did was to put the clock right again and then have a last word outside his mother's door before going to bed.

"Now I suggest that the following conversation took place next morning when he saw his mother.

"'About those noises we heard, mother. Did you think yo heard a dog?'

"'I didn't. But what made you say that?'

"'I don't know. I thought I heard one outside perhaps. An dogs terrify me. They make my hair rise, just as spiders an snakes do to some people.'"

Wharton nodded. Travers resumed.

"That told him she didn't hear the dog. What she may hav heard faintly through the thick wall was the dog scratching th bed or moving about the room when it woke up. But after tha Carne could put ideas in his mother's mind and establish th alibi. The more the two were questioned, the stronger the alib became.

"Now we go back to supposition again, and what happene at Montage Court. Try to think of the dramatic irony that wa brooding over the place that horrible night. That Borgia crea ture of a Sonia gloating over the doped figure of her husban and then slipping down to the door to let Carne in as arranged It was to be *their* wedding night, George; the consummation o revenge against Sidley. Together the two had a look at Sidley Everything, as Carne saw, had gone off well. So to the embraces Now do you see the mind that conceived *Pink Pearls?* You se him leaning over her, then the quick push of the knife aroun which he had pressed Sidley's fingers?

"Then Carne had to work quickly. His scheme was for Sidle to have murdered his wife, and then hanged himself after tak ing the dope to give him courage or deaden his brain. Carne' scheme was a better revenge against Sidley than anything Soni could have dreamed of. He put up the rope he had brought wit him and used Sidley's own shoes when he stood on the chair Then he realized to his horror that Sidley's body was too heav to haul, and the scheme had to be changed. But the alternative as he saw, would do as well. It would be assumed that Sidley had over-doped himself before he could hang himself. After tha Carne did all the rest of the jiggery-pokery and hunted the plac for any prints he might have left when he wasn't wearing gloves There was still plenty of time when he left the bedroom but un rtunately for him, Coales had set the alarm a bit early, and the host episode had to occur." He shook his head. "And that, I think, is the whole story."

"There's a lot in it," Wharton said. "My own idea is that she'd meant to have Sidley hanged. She was going to help put him in the noose, only Philip stabbed her first. By the way, I suppose Philip should have been hidden somewhere handy when Coales came in, so as to enjoy the full joke. He'd have been under the bed while Sonia was complaining to Coales about her sot of a husband." Then he clicked his tongue. "No use supposing things, though. It only lands you in a muddle."

Then the phone suddenly rang. The stenographer came in at the first sound and Travers took off the receiver. Wharton heard this:

"Yes? . . . Oh, good morning, Mrs. Carne. . . . Really? But you're sure? . . . Very well, then. I'm afraid there is some truth in . . . . Sorry, but I daren't. . . . No, I daren't. . . . You should know, Mrs. Carne. . . . I mean that you might have seen something suspicious about your car the next morning. . . . I daren't say more. . . I daren't, I tell you. Good-by."

A nod to the stenographer and Travers was back.

"You heard who that was, George. His mother, and I'll wager he knows. He's rung her up and said the police may be down here but it's all ridiculous. I should also say he put her on to ringing me up."

"And that bit about the car?"

"Only more bluff." He looked up. "Why can't you arrange to do something to her phone or his? Surely you could do some listening in?"

"I daren't do it," Wharton said. "There's been a goodish bit of the *agent provocateur* stuff already. We don't want any more Josey Parkers getting up in Parliament and asking questions. By the way, any chance of early lunch? If so, do you keep that stenographer in the kitchen while I do some phoning." He stopped. "One minute, though. Why not give Carne another message? Tell him about us and the dog. I'll listen in myself."

"That you, Carne?" Travers said. "Listen, quick! Why th
devil didn't you see you weren't followed when you buried tha
dog again?"

A gasp. "What do you mean?"

"Just got word the police dug it up at Carter's Wood. No
don't talk—listen! There's a conference going on this afternoo
and they'll be after you some time tonight. Unless—"

"Unless what?"

"I can't tell you now. Ring you some time later."

"Why didn't you let him talk?" Wharton said.

"If I didn't talk quickly myself, I'd be giving the game away,
Travers said. "This is getting a rather nervy business for me
George."

Wharton occupied that phone for over half an hour, and s
quietly did he speak that hardly a sound was heard in the kitch
en. At half-past twelve Palmer had lunch on. Wharton concen
trated on the meal and his thoughts, and when he pushed asid
his plate and rose, it was not to the fire that he was going, bu
for his hat and coat.

"I didn't want to spoil your meal," he said, "but the Power
That Be say we've got to drop tackling Carne." His lip curled
"They say there'll be an unholy row if it gets out."

Travers stared. "They're letting him get away with it?"

"They want everything done nice and proper," Wharton said
"We're to find how he acquired the dog, if you please. Build up a
certain case before we make a definite move."

He gave a sign for Travers to follow him out to the corridor
His voice lowered.

"I've warned you officially according to instructions. Now
you're a private person." He winked.

"I shall be at the Yard. If anything turns up, I'll warn you."

But Travers was far too annoyed at that display of officia
red-tape to do any pulling of chestnuts out of the fire, even fo
George Wharton. He was not aware, for one thing, of the ful
powers of the Commissioner, and for all he knew, Carne's wir
might by now be tapped and all conversations overheard. Bu
he sat on before the fire and as he began pondering the next of

ficial move, he all at once wondered why Philip Carne should be having any trust whatever in himself after that warning Patrick must have given him. But perhaps it was the other way; indeed it must be the other way. Patrick had mentioned that Travers for once had done the decent thing and had seemed to be siding against the police.

The stenographer was dismissed and Travers sat moodily over the fire again. Tea-time was drawing near when the phone bell rang again. It was Carne.

"That you, Travers?" His voice was under control and the sneering laugh rang true. "Is the little joke all over?"

"Sorry, but I'm doing no more talking," Travers said.

"Oh, but do let me tell you the truth about the dog! . . . Are you there? . . . Well, I've been leading you all on—"

"Sorry," Travers said again, "but I'm not listening, Carne. The next time you and I talk together will be at the Old Bailey."

He hung up and once more sat moodily gazing at the fire. Tea came in and dusk was in the sky before the phone bell went again. This time it was Wharton.

"That you, Mr. Travers? I'm speaking from a call-box." His voice was so mysterious that Travers could see him look over his shoulder as he talked. "Anything from Carne?"

"He's getting his courage back," Travers said. "He's making out it's a joke, and the laugh's on his side."

"Right," Wharton said. "Ring him up—unofficially—and hint that Coales has done some talking. Give him an hour and then stir him up with something else. We've got to get him to bolt. That's our only chance. Not a word to a soul. You understand."

But again it was Carne who did the phoning. Now his voice had a snarl in it.

"Is that you, Travers? I thought I'd let you know I've seen through your little game. Pretending you're getting information and every time I call you, you're in your flat."

"Have it your own way," Travers told him evenly.

"I'll have it my own way, all right. You always were a conceited swine, you know, Travers."

"Maybe," said Travers, "but the glasses I wear are genuine ones." Foolish, he thought, but it had made Carne think. "Now if you're still there, Carne, you'd better get hold of Coales and do your sneering at him. You never guessed he'd recognized you that night."

He rang off then, ashamed of himself for the lie. A dirty game, he thought, though Wharton would merely call it bluff. And yet perhaps the scruples were the hallmark of the conceited swine that Carne had called him. No matter what the weapons were when dealing with a mental pervert, an egomaniac and a murderer like Carne.

Dusk was in the sky when the phone rang again, and this time it was Norris. He said that a light had gone on in Carne's room, otherwise there was nothing to report, except perhaps that everything was in hand for a nation-wide inquiry about fawn Pekinese.

Dinner came and Travers left half the meal untouched. Then at about nine, Wharton rang, and the call was evidently another surreptitious one.

"Did you call him, Mr. Travers?"

"He called me," Travers said. "He's getting nasty-tempered."

"He is?" A quick excitement was in his voice. "Tell you what then. You ring him up just once more. He's still in his room. I'm now going back to the Yard."

So Travers called Carne's number, but strange to say, nothing happened. A mistake in the number, he thought, and dialed more carefully. Again nothing happened, and then suddenly he knew. In a moment he was ringing the Yard. Norris answered.

"Norris, Carne's flat's dead," Travers said urgently. "That light of his is a blind. He's bolted!"

"Right!" snapped Norris. "I'll get things going, sir, and you get here as soon as you can."

But when Travers reached the Yard Wharton had gone and Norris was a minute or two before he appeared.

"Carne won't get far, sir," Norris said as he got in the car. We don't mind if he does run loose for a day or two. It'll make things look all the worse."

Travers was curiously quiet and Norris shot him a look. Then as the car slipped along he began making conversation.

"Reason I kept you waiting, sir, was something I was just listening to. You know there've been some pictures stolen the last year or two. Well, they've just turned up."

"You mean, sent by the thief?"

"That'd be it, sir," Norris said, and drew up the car at the red light. "They can never get away with that game, sir. Pictures like that are too well known."

The car moved on again, turned left, then right, and was drawing up at the curb. A small group of sight-seers had gathered and a constable stood by the outer door. Sergeant Lewis came out, and a man with him.

"How'd you come to let him go?" Norris said.

Lewis's lip drooped. "He ain't gone, sir. He's up there in the chair. Did himself in.

"Dead!"

"Dead as dammit," Lewis said. "Stinking of cyanide. The Super's up there now."

Norris gave a nod. "Lost his nerve, did he? Well, I'm not grumbling." He turned, then stared. "Where's Mr. Travers?"

But Travers had gone, moving behind the gathering crowd and down through Parcel Street. The first steps had been a kind of panic: the quick accusing thought that it had been himself who had killed Philip Carne, and then the horror of seeing him. But as he walked on he began to see things more clearly. Wharton had been bluffing about making Carne bolt. He had had that suicide in mind from the very first. Now Travers could see him looking down at Carne's sprawling body and making his own complacent epitaphs.

Then Travers shook his head. And why not? The case was over and Wharton had got his man. And he had beaten those mystic bugbears of his—the Powers That Be. Travers smiled. A shrewd one, Wharton. Worth two of himself when it came to the final stages of the game. Churlish of himself, as well as cowardly running away like that, and it might be as well to go back and offer a congratulatory word.

So Travers stepped from the curb and then drew quickly back as the paper-van nipped by him. On its display boards the placards shrieked:

EXTRA—SPECIAL!! ——— **STOLEN PICTURES SENSATION!** ———	**EXTRA—SPECIAL!!** ——— **ROMNEY RETURNS!** ———